D0511680

LEABHARLANN CHONTAE ROSCOMAIN

DATE DUE	DATE DUE	DATE DUE	DATE DUE
18. JAN 03	03. NOV 04		
20. MAR 03	13. DEC 05		
03. 12. 0			
	31.		
31. DEC 03			
06. 01 04			
19. MAY 04			

they find the wolf, will rifle bullet, machete and dynamite be a match for the notorious El Lobo?

SRH

Vgu

good

THE KILLING OF EL LOBO

by

Elliot Conway

Dales Large Print Books
Long Preston, North Yorkshire,
BD23 4ND, England.

British Library Cataloguing in Publication Data.

Conway, Elliot
    The killing of El Lobo.

    A catalogue record of this book is
    available from the British Library

    ISBN   1-84262-181-5 pbk

First published in Great Britain 2001 by Robert Hale Limited

Copyright © Elliot Conway 2001

Cover illustration © Faba by arrangement with
Norma Editorial

Published in Large Print 2002 by arrangement with
Robert Hale Limited

Dales Large Print is an imprint of Library Magna Books Ltd.

Printed and bound in Great Britain by
T.J. (International) Ltd., Cornwall, PL28 8RW

For my *bueno amigos* of the
Barnard Castle Writers Circle

One

Gino Zarlarzo, *bandido* jefe, known and feared along both sides of the Rio Grande as El Lobo, the Wolf, was doing some heavy thinking as he led his trail-dust-raising band of killers deeper into the Mexican State of Chihuahua along the west bank of the Conchos.

Their latest raid into Texas had been fruitless. No gringo cattle or horses taken, no gringo women despoiled. He and his *muchachos* had only managed to escape being gunned down by a strong troop of Texas Rangers by swimming their horses across the Rio Bravo, the border river the Yankees called the Rio Grande.

Naturally his men were disappointed at not having any stolen gringo stock to sell, giving them the *dinero* to spend in the *cantinas* and whorehouses in Chihuahua City. And it was possible, El Lobo thought uneasily, his boys could be so upset they could be thinking of picking themselves another, more successful *jefe*, after they had shot him in the back. After all, it was the way he had become the *hombre* who said how things should be done, and took the biggest cut of all they stole.

A smile crept over El Lobo's fleshy, pock-marked face, as cold-blooded-looking as his four-legged namesake's fearsome, grimacing snarl as it went in for the kill. Away to his left, along the bank of the Conchos, he could see the high, pointed silhouette of a church steeple and the houses of the village of El Oro, a village they had not raided before.

While the spoils would not be as rich as those taken from raiding gringo ranches there would be women and tequila for the taking. Enough of both to take his *muchachos'* minds off thinking he was no longer fit to be their *jefe*. He pointed to the village, then took off his gold-braided peaked hat and lashed his horse's flanks with it. *'Adelante, muchachos!'* he yelled, all wolf now.

Old Juan Guereca, sitting outside his splay-timbered hut on the outskirts of El Oro, watching over his herd of goats, saw the trail dust of many riders closing in fast on the village. He knew it couldn't be an Apache warband; those red devils didn't show themselves until they were within bow-shot. Too late to do anything about it but to gabble out a prayer before the arrow or the cruel knife cut into your flesh.

Yet he knew the riders' intentions were the same as any Indians': they had come to kill, rape and burn. He had reasoned that if the horsemen were Federales they would have been riding in military double-file order, not in a ragged line. They could only be *bandidos*, and here, in northern Chihuahua, that meant El Lobo and his band of cut-throats. Guereca shivered. The Devil's own spawn was about to descend on the village of El Oro.

There was no time to alert the villagers of the fearful fate that was about to befall them. Even if there was, machetes and the few old rifles the villagers possessed wouldn't drive off El Lobo and his wolf pack. But there was time to warn Señora Deluva, the wife of the tall gringo, Langley, who was in Texas fighting in a big war. Guereca always thought gringos were loco; Señor Langley, the tall gringo, more so, to leave the warm-blooded Mexican widow he had married, who had borne him two fine boys, to go and risk his life in a war. Señor Langley had been a Texas Ranger and

9

Guereca thought that he would have had his fill of fighting and killing. Though he should not pass judgement on the crazy ways of a gringo. He had left a wife and young family to fight for the Juarista cause, to free Mexico from the French yoke.

Guereca picked up his rifle, only fit to be used against wild dogs and wolves now, and heaved himself on to his feet and headed as fast as his stiff-jointed legs would allow him, to the farm of Señora Deluvina Langley. He didn't get far on his mission.

He tumbled head over ass as he was making his way down the loose stone bank of the arroyo that ran like a knife slash across his piece of grazing land. He fell heavily and let out a groan as a stab of pain shot up his left leg. He tried to get back on to his feet, using his rifle as a crutch, but couldn't make it and had to drop down on his back again. Grimacing with pain, Guereca cursed. It felt as though he had broken or badly sprained his ankle. By the time he had crawled his way to the *senora's* farm, El Lobo and his butchers could have put the whole of El Oro to the torch.

Through tear-blurred eyes, Guereca saw the boy, Panchito, looking down at him from the opposite bank of the arroyo. No one had known the boy when he had come staggering into the village, more dead than alive a year ago. Only by discovering the boy had had his tongue cut out did the villagers realize he had been taken by the Apache and used as a slave.

The *señora* had taken the boy in as an addition to her family, naming him Panchito. When not working on the farm, Panchito fetched and carried for him and made sure his goats didn't wander too far away.

'Panchito!' he shouted, pointing along the arroyo. *'Bandidos!* Warn the *señora!'* He saw Panchito wasn't moving. 'Vamoose, boy! *Pronto!'*

Panchito glanced over his shoulder and saw the riders, heard their bubbling high-pitched whoops and yells. He clapped his hands over his ears to cut out the fearful sounds, reliving the terrible events when *bandidos* took him after killing his mother and father and burning down his home.

Then came the life of fear and pain as a slave of the Apache. The cutting off of his tongue, the daily struggle to find scraps of food around the Apache camp. Now men were riding in to kill and burn again. Panchito's sobs came out as a series of body-shaking grunts. Although Señora Langley had been like a mother to him and he knew her fate would be as terrible as his own parents' deaths had been, he lacked the will to run to the farm to tell her and his friends, her two boys, to run away and hide. All he wanted to do was to bury himself in some hole until the killings were over.

Guereca sank back, sighing as Panchito went from his sight. He had done his best for the family of the tall gringo, whom he thought could be long since dead. As he would be by the hands of El Lobo if he didn't get himself under cover. He suffered some more pain and began cursing again as he squeezed under a savage-thorned bush. Prayers he hadn't said for over fifty years came babbling from his lips as he heard the thunder of hooves, yelling and pistol shots and the *bandidos* rode along the rim on the arroyo to strike at the village. It was too late, even for a miracle, to help the villagers now.

Panchito, covered in dirt, crept cautiously out of the brush-screened hole on the bankside. The sun had moved well round; he must have been sheltering in the hole for four or five hours. He could no longer hear any yells or sounds of gunfire so he opined the *bandidos* had taken what they had wanted in the village and had ridden off.

Plucking up courage, he made his way, warily, along the edge of the river, keeping the bank between him and the village in case he had misjudged the *bandidos*' actions. Panchito scrambled out of the arroyo opposite where the *señora's* farm lay, to find his worst fears justified.

What could be burnt on the farm was a smoking, smouldering ruin. A horror-stricken Panchito walked slowly towards the destroyed buildings as though in a deep trance. His foster mother lay on her back, legs apart, clothes ripped and flung over her head, exposing the nakedness of her lower body. He could see no sign of the two boys. He sank to his knees, his sobs strangled howls of anguish. He had lived through the horrors the *señora's* sons would suffer. And he had been too scared to try and save them.

Wiping the tears from his eyes, Panchito got to his feet. The *señora* would have to be made decent, then he would bury her. That was the least he could do for the woman who had taken him in and treated him as one of her family, a boy who couldn't speak, and was more Apache than Mexican.

Panchito had wrapped up the *señora's* body, gently, in a partly scorched blanket and was hacking, wildly, at the hard ground with the only tool he could find, a smoke-blackened machete, the iron spike where the handle had been still warm to the touch.

He paused in his digging for a moment, to clear the sweat from his vision, and saw the *bandido* struggling from out of a hollow in the ground in front of him. The *bandido*, a fat-bellied man, burdened down with two bandoliers of rifle shells across his chest, came towards him, unsteady-legged, scowling-faced, clutching a bottle of tequila in his right hand. For a moment or two, Panchito froze in terror, then he saw the *bandido's* flies were open and Panchito knew he was looking at one of the men who had abused the *señora* and was now too drunk to realize his *compadres* had left. Something snapped inside him.

Mad-eyed, screeching wildly, he leapt at the *bandido* swinging the machete before the *bandido* could defend himself. A thick red flood spurted out of the awesome gash in the *bandido's* throat. As the fast-dying man sank to the ground, Panchito kept slashing at him with the machete.

Guereca, hands and face scratched and bloody, pinned Panchito's arms to his side. 'The pig is dead, Panchito!' he cried. 'Do

14

not waste any more of your strength on him! Use it to dig Señora Langley a proper grave!' He held him until he felt the fever-like shaking of Panchito stop. Judging that the boy's madness had run its course, he stood back and looked down at him, grim-faced.

'You are an *hombre* now, Panchito,' he said. 'You have faced a mad dog of a man and killed him, close enough to see the fear in his eyes. I am an old Juarista, yet I was too frightened to even gaze on the *bandidos*. You have shamed me, *amigo*. Now come and let us see to the *señora*.'

As they dug the grave, Guereca thought it would be merciful if the tall gringo had been killed in battle. It would save him much heartache if he never returned to El Oro.

Two

'Are you ridin' with us, Mart?' Lew Downing said. 'There's talk that General Shelby is here in Mexico and he's recruitin' ex-Rebs. He's hopin' to raise up a guerilla force big enough to cross back over the Rio Grande and show those Yankee carpetbaggers who are swarmin' into Texas that the South ain't licked yet. Most of the boys here are aimin' to join up. What about you, Sarge?'

Mart Langley, a tall, whipcord thin, solemn-faced Texan, shook his head. 'I quit bein' a sergeant,' he said, 'the day ole Bob Lee signed that peace treaty at Appomatox Courthouse, Lew. That day, like the general, I opined I'd had a bellyful of fightin' and killin', and riskin' bein' killed. Ain't you boys seen enough Texas blood spilt up at Gettysburg when General Hood sent us walkin' across the corn fields to try and chase the blue-bellies off Cemetery Ridge?'

Mart looked at the dozen or so Confederate soldiers crowded in the small *cantina* in the border town of Ojinaga in the Mexican

State of Chihuahua. Gaunt, wasted-faced men, ragged-garbed, some still wearing dirty, bloodstained bandages. Men who had fought and bled for a cause now lost forever, but were too stubborn proud to accept that they had been beaten.

He had accepted it, though he had never believed in the cause for which the South had destroyed itself. He had lived in Mexico for almost ten years, but when he had heard that Texas had lined up with the Confederacy he had ridden north to stand for his State. He could do no less. As a Texas Ranger, he had fought the enemies of the Lone Star State; Mexican, Indian, home-grown bandits, since the earliest days of the Republic.

'If you wild-asses ain't got rid of all your fightin' spirit,' he said, 'you cross the river to Presido. There's a Ranger post there. They'll welcome you with open arms. The pay ain't much, though that ain't anything new, but they'll feed you and supply you with ammunition for your guns. For that they'll expect you to withhold the law in this part of Texas. By what I gathered ridin' here, every ranch and farm along the border has been hit by raiders, and I don't mean Yankees. It's open season for any broncos, Mex or Injun, in Texas right now.' Mart smiled. 'But, bein' ornery Texans, I figure you ain't about to take note of me, so good luck to y'all wherever you end up, and keep your stupid heads low. I'm headin' south to my family, to tend my goats and sheep.'

'Tend goats and sheep?' Lew exclaimed in disbelief. 'And you pass yourself off as a Texan?'

'Yeah, woollies and goats,' replied Mart. 'I know that kinda jars with you longhorn men, but it's a damn site easier on the nerves than dodgin' blue-belly mini balls and cannon shot.'

'You'll get no disagreement on that observation, Mart,' Lew said. 'But an *hombre* has to do what he thinks he oughta.'

Even if it gets an *hombre* killed, Mart thought, but said, 'If you boys get some sense, my place is forty miles south of here, El Oro. Just follow that river runnin' past here and you'll not miss it. You'll be welcome to share what I've got until you sort yourselves out.'

Then, wishing all his former *compadres* good luck again, Mart left the *cantina* to mount up to ride south to see the family he had left two years ago. To a life of peace, so he could start to forget the bloody hell he had been lucky to come through unharmed.

Three

Mart, still up on his horse, face expression-less as though hewn from stone, looked down at the heap of dirt and stones, and the rough carved wooden cross. He didn't cry or beat at his breast in uncontrollable anguish on seeing his wife's grave and the manner of her dying, and the terrible fate of his two sons. Mart wasn't a man who showed his emotions openly. As a Ranger, and during the war, he had seen death and pain to those close to him in all its forms, knew that tears, prayers, curses couldn't alter that which had already happened.

That didn't mean he held no hatred for the men who had heaped all this pain and grief on him. His hatred was the cold, dedicated hatred of a man, come what may, who would get his revenge. El Lobo had signed his own death warrant, Mart thought, grimly. Even if it took him the rest of his life. After all, there was nothing here in El Oro for him now.

'I'm obliged, Señor Guereca, for seeing

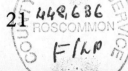

my woman decently buried,' he said. Mart cast a curious-eyed glance at the young boy standing along-side the old goat-herder. A thin-limbed, drawn-faced boy, only a few years older than his eldest boy had been. And whose old eyes held depths of pain and suffering a young boy should never have.

'This young *hombre* is Panchito, Señor Langley,' Guereca said proudly. 'He was the only one in the village who killed one of the *bandidos*. Killed him here with that machete he is carrying.'

Mart looked at the heavy-bladed cane knife hanging on the end of a piece of rope looped over the boy's narrow shoulders. He didn't think the boy had the strength to lift the machete, let alone cut a man to death with it.

'He killed one of the pigs who abused the *señora*,' Guereca added, then tears began to run down his leathery cheeks. 'I could do nothing.'

Panchito's neck ached with having to crane it to look up at the tall gringo's face. He had been frightened that the *señor* would be angry with him and old Guereca for not preventing the *bandidos* from killing his wife and stealing his sons. He had thought that he would pull out one of his big pistols and shoot them both dead. Panchito had never seen a gringo before, but by what he had heard in the village, the Texas gringos were *mal hombres* and hated all Mexicans, whom they called 'greasers'.

Panchito could see no anger in the tall gringo's face as he looked him straight in the eyes. His face seemed to grow longer, harder. Panchito shivered. Like the Apache, the tall gringo would make a bitter and merciless enemy.

Mart was doing some shivering of his own. Guereca had told him about Panchito being captured by the Apache and having his tongue cut out. The same fate could be waiting for his two boys. It would have been better if they had been killed in the raid then they could have been laid to rest alongside their mother.

'When you ride out on your vengeance trail, Señor Langley,' Guereca said, 'and it is written in your face that you are seeking to kill El Lobo, I and Panchito will ride with you. We, as you Texans say, are beholden to you. There is nothing for us here, the *bandidos* shot the goats they did not take. Who in the village will see that Panchito is fed, now that your *señora* is dead? The young *hombre* will not be a burden on the trail,

23

señor; he has already proved himself and he is a good tracker.'

Mart stopped worrying about what could be happening to his boys and got to thinking of what had to be done, the hunting down and the killing of El Lobo. He looked down at the grim, determined faces of the two beholden *hombres*, one of them in his seventies, the other a half-wild boy. It didn't seem a formidable force to take on a large gang of killers. Yet the alternative was to track down El Lobo on his own. Although he was more than a fair hand at reading sign he wasn't a one-man army.

The old man, Mart reasoned, knew about killing. He had fought against the French and knew his way round Chihuahua, the boy had also been blooded. He guessed that Panchito craved friendly company, to be accepted as an *hombre* with a purpose in life that would take his mind off his disability. Helping to kill *bandidos* would certainly do that for him, and also get him dead, Mart thought, soberly.

He smiled, '*Amigos*,' he said, 'it will be an honour to have you ride at my side. Though you have to understand the three of us could end up dead in a day or two.'

Panchito lost his haunted look and he

smiled up at the tall gringo. Guereca's toothless grin signified his acceptance; he had no fears of an early grave.

'We're headin' for Texas, *hombres*,' Mart said. 'El Lobo raids across the Rio Bravo, the Rangers at Presido should give us some intelligence of where his band crossed back into Mexico then m'be we can pick up the bastard's trail to his hole-up. It's a long shot, but it's better than scoutin' all along the river to try and cut his sign, or meet the whole bunch of them head-on. And those are odds we don't want.'

Mart looked at the burro and Guereca's ancient single-shot rifle and the boy's machete. He smiled. 'We'll stop at Ojinaga before we cross into Texas, *amigos*. As well as gettin' us some supplies and a pack horse, I'll get you both a rifle and a pistol plus a horse apiece. We're aimin' to make a fight of it, not contemplate suicide.'

Mart took a final look at his wife's grave, and the blackened ruins of what had once been his home, then said, 'OK, *compadres*, mount up; there's nothin' here now for any of us.'

Four

There were still bunches of ex-Confederate soldiers wandering about at a loss in Ojinaga when Mart and his *compadres* rode in. He noticed several men, not in uniform, lounging in the shade of a *cantina* porch: shut-faced, taking men. He had no difficulty in placing them as border ruffians; cattle-lifters, stage-heisters, men happy to kill to get their wherewithal. As a Ranger, he had chased after the trail-dust of many suchlike men.

Mart drew up his horse outside the largest general store in the town and dismounted. 'I would like you inside with me, Señor Guereca,' he said. He grinned. 'Just to make sure the storekeeper doesn't try to cheat a gringo. You, Panchito, stay with the mounts. There's *hombres* here mean-minded enough to steal them. Any trouble you come in runnin', OK?'

Panchito's OK was a quick bob of his head.

On a makeshift counter, planks laid across

crates on the far side of the store, Mart saw a display of pistols, rifles and belts of reloads that would almost arm a troop of cavalry. Guns, he opined, sold by the dispirited ex-Rebs for food, liquor, or the pleasures of bouncing a *cantina señorita* in the private rooms. Through the open door at the rear of the store he also saw several horses running loose in a small corral. Mart gave a grunt of satisfaction. If the storekeeper wasn't a hard bargainer his two 'Rangers' would have slightly more favourable odds of staying alive along the vengeance trail on which they were about to embark.

Lopez, the storekeeper, silently cursed his two new customers; a tall horse-faced gringo and an old stoop-backed compatriot, carrying a rifle as old as himself. Surely, Lopez thought, sunken-hearted, the old bastard wasn't expecting him to hand over good Yankee dollars for an ancient weapon like that just because he was Mexican?

It had been a heavy buying few days for Lopez, buying guns and cartridges from gringo ex-soldiers in numbers he had no hope of selling in Ojinaga. The only Mexicans who would be interested in owning good quality Yankee guns were El Lobo and his troop of cut-throats. And they wouldn't trade; they would just come ass-kicking it in and take them, after shooting him dead.

Yet he had to buy whatever the Texan soldiers offered for sale. They were *hombres* who had come through the bloody hell of a big war and lost all but their lives and what they had on their backs. Hair-triggered-tempered men who, at any refusal on his part to trade cash for guns or whatever, would burn down his store about his ears. What chewed at his guts most was that the Yankee sons-of-bitches were spending his hard-come-by dollars in the town's *cantinas*, not in his store. Lopez felt like bursting into tears at the injustice of it all. He willed his face to show a trader's welcoming smile at his customers. Hopefully he said, 'Supplies, *señor?*'

'Yeah,' Mart replied. 'I want two repeating rifles, two pistols, and reloads. And a coupla horses with all their gear. And supplies: coffee, beans, bacon, grain for the horses. Enough for three for m'be a week on the trail. And you'd better throw in a bag of flour and some sugar.' He thin-smiled at the storekeeper. 'Providin' you ain't about to drive a hard bargain with a gringo, *señor.*'

Lopez's smile hotted up; he was selling something at last. '*Señor,*' he said with some feeling, 'you will not find any lower prices in the whole of Chihuahua. May the Buenos Dios strike me down in this place if I do not tell the truth. I will get your supplies; you pick your guns and horses, *señor*.'

Mart and Guereca strode across to the gun counter and began examining the weapons. Mart picked up a short-barrelled, fifteen-load Winchester carbine. He passed it over to Guereca. 'Will the boy be able to manage this?' he asked.

The old Mexican smiled. 'He has never owned a gun before, Señor Langley, but he will learn fast, as we had to do at his age.' His smile froze as they both heard the sound of hoarse jeering laughter, then a pistol shot, and Panchito's alarmed gurgling cries.

Mart's face steeled over. He nodded towards the open rear door of the store. Guereca gave him an acknowledging nod back and grabbed a handful of shells for the carbine then moved to the opening at a speed that belied his age, almost knocking over the storekeeper in his haste to do his *jefe's* bidding.

Mart stepped out on to the front porch, pistol out and held down by his right leg. The three cold-visaged men he had seen in front of the *cantina* were now on the street, standing in a half circle around Panchito. The man holding the pistol fired again raising the dust only inches from Panchito's feet. Panchito jumped nervously but still retained his hold of the horse and mule's reins, wielding his machete with his other hand. And still having the courage to glare back fiercely at his tormentor.

The pistol man laughed. 'You ain't jumpin' high for a young greaser. M'be I ain't firin' close enough.' He drew back the hammer of his gun for another shot.

Mart's shot came first. The gunman let out a high-pitched howl of pain as the shell tore through his right foot, causing him to drop his pistol. Hopping on one leg, face twisted in agony, he swung round to face Mart. 'You sonuvabitch!' he shrieked. 'You've busted my foot! What the hell did you do that for?'

'I was just wonderin' if a gringo asshole could jump higher than a greaser kid,' Mart said, conversationally. Then, his voice hardening, he added, 'That boy is a *compadre* of mine. What you do to him you answer to me for, *comprende?*' He held his pistol steady on the wounded gunman, but didn't neglect to keep a watchful eye on the man's two *compadres*.

Mart's alertness hadn't been in vain. He glimpsed a flicker of movement from the gunman nearest to him and brought his pistol round fast, and triggered off a shot from across his belly. The man staggered back on his heels, hand still holding on to the butt of his undrawn pistol, then dropped, like a felled tree, to the ground, with a slow-spreading red stain marking the front of his vest.

Mart had no compunction in killing him. The gunman had taken a gamble and lost, for ever. It didn't pay a man to give his enemy a second chance to kill him.

Guereca jabbed the carbine into the back of the remaining gunman, making him wince with pain. 'Don't be so foolish as your *compadre, señor,*' he said. 'Or I'll have to kill my first gringo.'

The gunman did some rapid assaying. With a greaser jamming a rifle hard against his back-bone and a fast-shooting Yankee beanpole with a bead on him, he knew, if he didn't want to end up in the dirt dead like Billy, it was time to eat crow. 'You'll get no trouble from me, mister,' he said, then slowly raised his hands.

Mart hard-eyed him for a few moments but could see no signs on his face that he had been speaking forked-tongued words. 'A wise move, pilgrim,' he said. 'Now, get to your horse and leave town, pronto. Keep him covered with that carbine, Señor Guereca, just in case he starts thinkin' not-so-wise thoughts and wants to make a fight of it.' Then Mart's attention was distracted on hearing Panchito's choking cries. He spun round and saw the man he had wounded falling on to his face, eyes glazed and out of focus as he hit the ground, the small pistol he'd held in his hand lying in the open alongside him. And Panchito's machete buried deep in his back. Whatever doubts he'd had about allowing the boy to ride with him vanished. For the second time the boy had proved himself an *hombre*. Definitely a man whom he could trust to watch his back.

'I'm beholden to you now, Panchito,' he said. 'That fella would have gunned me down like a dog if you hadn't sharp eyes.' He bent down and picked up the derringer and put it in his pocket. 'Señor Guereca,' he said. 'Give the young hellion that carbine.' Mart watched a proud-smiling Panchito handling the gun, hefting it then bringing it up to his shoulder into a firing position. He grinned at the boy. 'If that other fella comes by this way lookin' like trouble you just cut loose at him. Bein' that you're new to a rifle you'll probably not hit him but you oughta scare him off.'

Panchito, still all smiles, nodded vigorously, then pulling a stern *hombre's* face held the rifle high across his chest.

'OK, Señor Guereca,' Mart said. 'Let's get this young *hombre* a horse and get ridin' outa here before he trees the town.'

The storekeeper cut his prices still further for the tall gringo. A gringo, an old Mexican and a young boy who couldn't speak were unusual trail *compadres* though that hadn't stopped them killing Texan bad-asses as efficiently as any border *pistolero*. He had no idea why they were riding together, but knew it would mean big trouble for someone. They made him feel uncomfortable and he wanted them out of his store as soon as he could without showing them any discourtesy in case the dumb *chico* flung his machete into his back.

An hour after the shootings, a well-kitted-out trio splashed their way across the Rio Grande to ride into the Texas border town of Presido.

34

Five

El Lobo's smile was almost human; his luck was riding high once more. He drew his horse back from the ridge and rode down to the foot of the rise to where his *muchachos* were waiting, their mounts' legs still damp and steaming from the crossing of the Rio Bravo.

El Lobo had seen at least 150 head of prime Texas longhorns bedded down at the creek running along the bottom of the valley on the other side of the ridge. They would be easily taken. All it needed, come dark, was for five or six of his boys to sneak into the gringos' camp and slit the throats of the Texans who were with the cattle.

It had to be a silent killing, gunfire would stampede the cattle, or bring a Texas Ranger patrol down about his ears. As soon as it broke light, his *muchachos* would drive the herd along, fast, and cross the Rio Bravo before any alarm was raised. The dollars he would get for the cattle, El Lobo thought, confidently, would ensure he still stayed *jefe*.

Josh Ritchie, one of the two night riders, stiffened up in his saddle, fully alert. He couldn't see, or hear, anything in the darkness other than the restless stirring and snorting of the cows, but his self-preservation instincts were raising the hair at the nape of his neck. Something wasn't quite what it seemed out there. A man who lifted cattle for a living developed suchlike extra senses, or ended up swinging from the hanging tree. Tensed-nerved he peered harder into the night, his pistol fisted.

Ritchie sensed rather than saw a slight movement at the side of him, then it seemed to him as though a piece of the darkness came up at him with a rush. Hands clawed at him and he felt the weight of a man's body on his back, heard his panting breath and the cold, prickly sensation of a knife blade nicking his neck.

Fright and anger drove all sleep and tiredness out of Ritchie. In one swift action, his feet were free of his stirrups and he was flinging himself out of the saddle, bringing his surprised attacker with him, half-turning in mid-air so that the man's body was beneath him as he hit the ground. He heard his assailant's grunting gasp as the breath was knocked out of him. He rolled on to his knees then, cursing and swearing, he battered at the man's head in a frenzied attack with his pistol until he lay limp and silent.

Ritchie stood up in a crouching position, panting and trembling, lips drawn back in a savage snarl, worked up into a killing mood. But no one else came at him from the dark. He began to think about who the hell were the men who were attacking his camp. They couldn't be Rangers; those sons-of-bitches, he thought, would have held off till daylight then ringed them in with rifles and called on him and his boys to surrender or be blown to Kingdom Come. Sneaking in the dark, like a bunch of hair-lifting Indians, wasn't their style at all. He bent down over the man he had pistol-whipped to death to discover by his garb he was a Mexican. 'Greasers!' he snarled.

Greaser *bandidos* were after the cattle he and his boys had risked their necks to lift. Yet he still couldn't hear any unusual sounds, no pistol shots, no yells of alarm from his boys, so he had to accept the worst; the grim fact that the Mexican throat-cutters had done their deadly work. Ritchie did some more cursing and was all set to fire his pistol and spook the cattle to prevent them from falling into the hands of the *bandidos* then had a quick second thought.

The whole camp would be crawling with them, he reasoned, and his pistol flash would draw them on to him and he would end up as dead as his boys were. Then how could he make the bastards pay in blood for stealing his cows? He couldn't dare show his face among the owlhoot fraternity in the border saloons unless he tracked them down, or died in doing so. He didn't want to be remembered as the man who allowed a bunch of greaser *bandidos* to sneak up on him as though he was an Eastern green-horn, cut his boys' throats and steal his cattle.

Suddenly, as though sprouting up from the ground, he saw the blurred shapes of riders all around him proving for certain the raiders were Mexican. No Texas cattle-lifter, and he was on nodding terms with most of them, ran a gang this big. It seemed that the best part of the Mexican army was milling about him.

Ritichie heard a name being called several times. Urbino, he thought, and guessed they were calling for the man he had killed. He dropped to the ground and, getting hold of the dead man's ankles, dragged him along behind him as he wormed his way into a clump of brush. There he waited, ready to take some of the raiders with him to Hell if they spotted him.

El Lobo quickly changed his mind about waiting until daylight to move the cattle. Urbino not showing up meant he was dead and one of the gringo pigs was alive, lying low somewhere in the darkness, a threat to them. The man could stampede the cattle and in the mad confusion while he and his *muchachos* were trying to keep clear of the trampling hooves and thrusting horns of the cattle, he could shoot some of them out of their saddles.

'*Muchachos*!' he yelled. 'We drive the cattle, pronto!' El Lobo waited until his men had positioned themselves around the herd then drew out his pistol and fired several shots into the air causing his own stampede, but heading in the direction he wanted, south.

Only after the sounds of the longhorns were just a faint drumming in the distance, did Ritichie get to his feet, coughing, spluttering, from the thick dust haze the spooked cattle had raised. He began calling out the names of his boys, hoping against hope they hadn't all been butchered, but heard no answering call. Hard-faced, he walked towards the camp; it was in darkness and he still tasted dust in the air. He could feel by the churned-up ground the herd had stormed through the camp, pounding to pieces everything in its path, men, guns and gear. Ritchie prayed that his men had died before that had happened. Fuelling his rage still further was the discovery that the horses were no longer tied up at the horse line.

Josh Ritchie dirty-mouthed the *bandidos* loud enough to have been heard clear to the Rio Grande. There was no way he would be able to get on the trail of them, he thought, angrily, without a goddamned horse, and to make matters worse he had no water or rations and was only armed with a six-load pistol.

Presido was the nearest town, but a long haul hoofing it. Showing up there would be like walking slap bang into a hangman's noose, the marshal there holding several warrants on him for cattle stealing. Ritchie opined he would take the chance of lifting a horse from some sodbuster's holding or a ranch before he made it to the Rio Grande. He gave a frozen-faced grin. The Rangers wanted to hang him for stealing longhorns; they couldn't hang him twice for horse-stealing.

Six

Mart and his *compadres* made their first camp on the trail twelve miles west of Presido. They had ridden slightly north-wards after leaving the border town, still keeping the Rio Grande within six or seven miles on their left flank. Mart hoped to cut the sign of a large band of riders either heading deeper into Texas, or hightailing back below the line, tracks which he knew could only be made by El Lobo's raiders, tracks clear enough to follow. His other hope for a lead, news of the latest sighting of El Lobo from the Rangers, had proved fruitless.

'We've had no recent intelligence of the whereabouts of that sonuvabitch, Mr Langley,' the Ranger captain at Presido had replied, when he had told him he was intending to hunt down the bandit.

'The only raidin' bein' carried out in the territory is by a warband of bronco Apache and I've got two patrols out tryin' to rope 'em in,' the captain continued. He cast a critical-eyed gaze at Mart and his two *compañeros* and spoke again. 'I don't wish to deter a man from doin' what he considers he has to do, Mr Langley, and no offence intended, but El Lobo and his wild boys will have the advantage if you do have a run-in with them.'

Mart favoured the captain with a lopsided grin. 'I ain't disputin' your opinion, Capt'n, though we ain't hankerin' on takin' on the whole of the gang. If we can get close enough to pull off a killin' shot at El Lobo me and my *amigos* will take with a good heart what the Good Lord has in store for us.'

The captain was still shaking his head at the craziness of some men as he watched the three ride out of the post. 'If they're unlucky enough to meet up with El Lobo,' he said to his sergeant, 'someone will have to start diggin' three graves.'

'Don't sell that tall *hombre* short, Capt'n,' replied the sergeant. 'He used to be a Ranger, a sergeant in fact, Sergeant Mart Langley.'

'*The* Sergeant Langley?' the captain said, sharply. 'I've heard of him all right. One of the best manhunters along the border, so talk had it.'

'It ain't just talk, Capt'n,' the sergeant said. 'Langley learnt his trade servin' under Captain Coffee Hays. Was with him way back in '41 at Plum Creek when the capt'n led a Ranger patrol of only twenty-five men agin over a hundred wild-ass Comanche, and whupped them. No sir, if there's a fella who can catch El Lobo in the sights of his Winchester, even with a Mex kid and his old grandpappy to back his play, it's Mart Langley. He knows his way around on both sides of the river, havin' lived in Chihuahua since he got himself hitched to a Mex woman when he left the service.'

It was with much more respect in his gaze the captain watched the hopeful hunters of El Lobo disappear in the shimmering heat-haze. Thinking he was in no position to ridicule Mr Langley's virtual one-man attempt to hunt down and kill the most notorious bandit in the South-west, he could do no worse than his company of Rangers had done so far in trying to capture El Lobo, which was sweet damn all.

A thirsty, footsore, Ritchie brightened up somewhat as he caught the smell of camp-fire smoke drifting in the breeze blowing from the direction of a small stand of cottonwoods away to his right. Moving closer to the trees, he saw tethered horses, three with saddles on them and a pack horse. He couldn't yet see the three owners at the camp. Too many for him to walk in and throw down on. It would have to be case of Indian-up on the horses and leave just as silently until out of rifle range, then ass-kick it for the Rio Grande, where, out of reach of the Texas lawmen he could plan just how he was going to gut-shoot El Lobo.

Ritchie also thought of taking the pack horse; whatever supplies it was loaded with would come in useful, though decided against it, being greedy could get him killed. He would be satisfied taking the rifle he could see sticking out of one of the packs it was carrying; the rifle boots on the three mounts were empty.

Mart sipped idly at his coffee, glancing now and again at Panchito. The boy had volunteered for the first watch and was sitting well away from the fire watching both the horse line and the trail. Straight-backed, holding his carbine in his right hand, butt on the ground, looking all *hombre*. Mart's face hardened; the boy had had no childhood: he would try his damnedest to make sure he had an adult life before him.

Old Guereca, sitting opposite him, had his hat tipped over his eyes, dozing, the dead stub of a cigarillo sticking to his lower lip. Like him, Mart thought, the old man had ceased to worry or fear about dying at the hands of El Lobo. Like the Indians, the Mexicans believed in what was already written would happen. Mart didn't believe in that way of thinking: he wanted to do some writing of his own as far as El Lobo was concerned.

Panchito's eyes narrowed and his grip on the stock of the carbine tightened. The long grass down by the horse line was moving against the wind. He didn't want to look foolish in the eyes of his *jefe*, the tall gringo, by raising an alarm when it could be only a trick of the wind blowing through the trees. It could well be that, Panchito thought, but he had lived long enough with the Apache to know it was wiser to check out anything that seemed unusual.

Mart brought his ruminating gaze back on to Panchito to find the boy wasn't there. He smiled. The boy was more Indian than Mexican when it came to moving around. He took it that the boy had gone into the trees to relieve himself.

Ritchie, sweating with the exertion of belly-crawling twenty yards or so through the tall thick grass, and apprehension, allowed himself a congratulatory smile. He had the horses between himself and the camp without being detected, so he judged it safe to get to his feet. He didn't want to cause a commotion among the horses by suddenly appearing out of the ground right under their noses.

Ritichie made for the rifle on the pack horse, taking only two steps when he felt something hard and round dig into his back. He cursed silently. He didn't need a Western Union wire to tell him it was a rifle muzzle boring into his ribs. What did surprise him as he twisted his head round, was that the man who had jumped him wasn't a man at all, but a skinny greaser kid, half the size of him. Ritchie's spirits rose. He wasn't between a rock and a hard place yet.

He raised his hands and turned slowly round, smiling, ready to swing his arms down fast and knock the rifle out of the kid's hands then cold-cock the little bastard with his pistol for scaring him.

'There ain't no need to point that long gun at me, sonny,' he said. Then Ritchie's fork-tongued smile twisted into a rictus-like grimace and his sweet-talking dried up in his throat.

Ritchie was familiar with killing looks; he had shown a few fish-eyed looks of his own in his time, and he was eyeballing one now. The kid was favouring him with a blood-crazy look that would have chilled the blood of a hair-lifting Apache. He had no doubt that the kid would take great delight in blowing a big hole right through him if he so much as broke wind. He raised his hands real high and tried to fix his face into a regular smile, but he found he had no control over his face muscles.

Panchito reached out with one hand and yanked out the pistol belted across the gringo's fat belly and slipped it down the top of his pants then jabbed him again with his rifle, jerking his head in the direction of the camp. Ritchie turned and did what he wanted him to – doing some more silent cursing at his run of bad luck. First a greaser *bandido* had killed his boys and stolen his cattle, and now a half-pint greaser kid had him well and truly by the balls. That big rock was pressing hard in his back.

'Well I'll be durned!' Mart exclaimed, as he saw Panchito herding the big man into the camp. He got to his feet and drew his pistol. 'We're gettin' too old for this man-huntin' lark,' he said to Guereca. 'The boy's saved us from lookin' like a coupla fools, saved our lives m'be. Scout around and see if the sonuvabitch has any buddies close by.'

Guereca spat out the soggy butt of the cigarillo and picked up his rifle and cut off away from the fire to circle the trees, ready to shoot on sight any gringo he saw sneaking around behind them.

Mart got another surprise when he saw who Panchito's prisoner was. 'Well, as I live and breathe, Josh Ritchie!' he gasped. 'I thought you'd have had your neck well and truly stretched by now. I've tasted you and your thievin' boys' trail-dust more times than I liked.' He smiled at Panchito. '*Bueno* work, Panchito,' he said. 'Are there any more suchlike *hombres* after the horses?'

Panchito, chest almost bursting with pride, shook his head.

'I'll keep an eye on this *hombre*,' Mart said. 'I'd be obliged if you'd go and bring in Señor Guereca.'

A scowling-faced Ritchie lowered his arms. 'I didn't know the Rangers hired old men and kids, greasers as well.' He shot a baleful look at Panchito, running towards the horse line. 'Where the hell did you get that bloodthirsty greaser kid from? He almost frightened the crap outa me, snuck up on me like a bronco Injun. The young sonuvabitch was itchin' to put a hole through me.'

'You'd better believe it, Ritchie,' replied Mart. 'That *greaser* kid has already killed two men with that machete he's totin'. I guess he was lookin' forward to killin' his first man, a hated gringo, with a gun. And I'd advise you not to upset him further by callin' him, and the old man, greasers. They're Mexicans, and proud of it. The boy was an Apache slave and some of their rough ways have rubbed off on him. Hurt his pride and he'll kill you. And I won't stop him.'

'He ain't exactly filled with the milk of human kindness, that's for sure,' growled Ritchie. Then, looking hopefully at Mart, he said, 'If you ain't a Ranger, does that mean you ain't gonna turn me in?'

'I'm on pressin' business, Ritchie,' Mart said. 'I can't waste time haulin' you to a Ranger post; that means goin' back to Presido. I take it that you're still in the cattle-lifting trade?' Mart's lips twitched in a ghost of a smile. 'Though by the look of you it don't seem very profitable. You look as though you've done some hard travellin'.'

'Hard walkin' is the word for it, Langley,' Ritchie snarled. 'I ain't got a horse, or a rifle and the only gear I've got is what you see I'm wearin'. If you'd allow me to sit down and help myself to some of that water in yonder canteen, and m'be a helpin' of those fine beans and coffee I can smell, then I'll tell you why that boy found me pussy-footin' around your horses.'

Both Guereca and Panchito had joined Mart and Ritchie at the fire, as the rustler was telling how he had lost his cows and the killing of his men. Panchito couldn't fully understand what the fat gringo was saying, but by the look on his *jefe* and the old man's face, it was of great interest to them.

'And you're convinced it was El Lobo's doin', Ritchie,' Mart said.

'As sure as I'm sittin' here drinkin' your coffee,' replied Ritchie. 'He's the only son-uvabitch along the border who runs a gang as big as the one who took my herd. I came here to steal me a horse and a rifle and start trackin' down El Lobo, that's how certain I am it was him who butchered my boys.' He smiled crookedly at Mart. 'M'be you're thinkin' I'm loco goin' after the Wolf on my own, but as well as you grea– you Mexi-

50

cans,' he said, 'we gringos have a measure of pride, even bad-ass gringos like me. That El Lobo spat in my eye and I aim to get even, or get myself killed.'

'If you're loco, Ritchie,' Mart said, 'then you're gazin' at three other crazies. We're on the same *hombre's* trail, El Lobo. And we're aimin' to dispatch him to Hell where he should have been sent a long time ago.'

Ritchie's eyes widened in surprise, though he thought they shouldn't have done. There would be dozens of men along the border territory who had a killing score to settle with the *bandido*. He had to admit not many of them would be mad enough to take action to settle up their grievances with El Lobo, unless they were at the head of one hell of a big posse. He wondered what had set the ex-Ranger backed up by an old man and a half-wild kid on El Lobo's trail, and was curious enough to ask why.

Mart's face Indianed over; harsh-voiced, he said, 'El Lobo paid a call on the village I lived in, across the river in Chihuahua, since I quit the Rangers. My wife was raped before they killed her. And my two boys took away to live through the hell young Panchito there suffered, as slaves of the Apache.' His smile was a frozen mask of hate. 'Oh we're loco all right, but it's a righteous madness, Ritchie.

'We ain't had any luck pickin' up the bastard's trail yet,' Mart continued. 'So we've a long way to go before I get the satisfaction of putting several Winchester loads in his dirty hide.'

Ritchie close-eyed Mart and his *compadres* for a few moments before speaking again. He knew of Mart's rep as a crack manhunter. He'd had the long-faced son-of-a-bitch breathing uncomfortably down his neck more times than he had liked, but he had never ridden with Mexicans before, though if the old man was as sharp as the kid, then the three of them were as good as any *pistoleros* he could hand-pick. That would make it four guns, still not a lot of firepower to go up against twenty, twenty-five hardcases, but a great deal better than his lone gun. That is if the kid gave him his gun back.

'I could be of some help on that score, Langley,' he said. 'Back a piece on the way I came, El Lobo left a good trail, made by my longhorns, and it ain't but a few hours old. Now if you *compadres* are willin' I'd like to join up with y'all.' He grinned at Panchito. 'I know me and the boy got off on the wrong foot, but I don't blame him for that. I don't know how much gringo talk he savvies but you can tell him from me, Langley, when he can jump one of the sneakiest sonsuvbitches along both sides of the border he's real *bueno*. Now the way I read it El Lobo is holdin' all the aces and I know that one extra gun ain't goin' to swing the odds a heap in our favour, but it's a start.' He looked Mart full in the eye. 'What do you say, Langley?'

Mart didn't have to think too hard over the rustler's willingness to ride with them. He would accept any help he could get to see El Lobo dead, providing the man offering his gun was capable of using it. Ritchie was a border hard man, a *pistolero*, an ally he was in no position to turn down. The fact that Ritchie was a law-breaker didn't matter, he was no longer a Ranger, and in his book the tracking down and dispatching of a killer like El Lobo came before the taking in of a cattle-lifter. First, though, it was only right and proper he should ask his *compadres* to state their opinion on whether or not they wanted another gringo to ride with them. He looked across at Señor Guereca. 'Do we ride as four?' he said.

The old Mexican hard-eyed Ritchie, a *mal hombre* with little time for greasers, until now. In a way, they were at war with El Lobo, though the *bandido jefe* didn't know it yet. Strange alliances had to be made to achieve victory in any war. The Juarista army had *peons, caballeros,* dons, even Indians in its ranks. He shrugged, expressively, and favoured Ritchie with another stone-eyed look. 'Who better than a cattle-thief to track down a cattle-thief, Señor Langley?' he said.

Panchito hadn't understood all the Yankee *bandido* had said, but had heard the word *bueno,* good, he'd used when looking at him. He could see no hatred in Ritchie's eyes against him for causing him to lose face. Señor Langley was asking for his advice as though he was a full-grown *hombre* and he had to think like one. Whether he liked the gringo *bandido* or not didn't matter, his two *compadres* wanted him to fight alongside them. That didn't mean he need not keep a watchful eye on him and, at the first signs of the *bandido* playing his *jefe* false, kill him. Panchito flashed that message to Ritchie in a fierce-eyed glare before he nodded his agreement for the *bandido* to join them.

Ritchie got the unspoken message. This

was the second time, he thought, the half-pint kid had given him the chills. He must be getting old. And he wouldn't be getting much older if he didn't win the kid's trust. If they were forced into a tight corner, each of them looking out for each other, he would feel more than a mite uneasy if he had someone who hated his guts to watch his back.

'That's settled then,' Mart said. 'Welcome to the camp, Ritchie. We'll spread the pack horse's load among our mounts, so that will give you a horse, and fix you up with a pistol and a long gun.' He grinned at the rustler. 'Though that'll mean you'll be ridin' bare-back like an Injun buck; we ain't got the time to go back to Presido to pick up a saddle.'

'*Amigos*,' Ritchie said, 'I'd ride bare-assed rather than hoof it any further, and that's the goddamned truth.'

Seven

Panchito came rib-kicking it back, drawing up his mount in a dust-raising halt in front of Mart and Ritchie. Face working excitedly, he pointed first to his right, then to the far distant purple blur of the mountain range behind him.

'The sonsuvbitches have split up, is that it, Panchito?' Mart said.

Even Ritchie's stone heart softened somewhat on hearing Panchito's fractured grunting which he took to be the kid's, 'Yes'. And he was a man who held no tender feelings towards man, woman, child, horse, or dog. Definitely not for any Mexican. What the kid had already gone through in his young life must have left him raw-nerved. Ritchie reckoned he had been lucky that the kid hadn't slashed him to pieces with his machete when he had jumped him at the horse line.

They were twenty miles south of the Rio Grande, following the well-beaten tracks of Ritchie's herd heading deeper into Chihuahua.

'It's like followin' a goddamned turnpike, Langley,' Ritchie said. 'We could trail these tracks clear to South America.'

'This is *bandido* territory, Ritchie,' Mart told him, 'El Lobo's bailiwick; there's no need to hide his tracks. The Federales know El Lobo's stronghold is somewhere in those mountains ahead. Even if they knew exactly in which valley or canyon he's bedded down in, it would take half the Mex Army, backed up by a battery of big guns to try to take him. But it would be a waste of men and powder. If things got too hot for El Lobo, why, he and his boys would melt away through the passes and over the ridges on the far side of the high country.'

Then Mart gave orders to old Guereca and Panchito to scout well ahead. 'Ride easy, *compadres*,' he said. 'As though you ain't in a hurry to make it to any place in particular. I figure that El Lobo won't drive the cattle into the mountains, he'll have a business deal with some local ranchero to take the cattle off his hands. Then we can pick up his trail as he rides for his hole-up.' He cold-smiled at his small army. 'From then on in, we'll have to be the four sneakiest *hombres* in the whole of Chihuahua. You send Panchito back, Señor

Guereca, when the tracks change. And if you run into *bandido* trouble, don't hang around, you both ride out of it fast, and we'll meet it together, OK?'

'OK, Señor Langley,' replied the old Mexican. He showed toothless gums in a wide smile. 'If I can hold back the young *pistolero* from wanting to taste more *bandido* blood.'

Mart and Ritchie rode along in silence, Ritchie opining that the ex-Ranger wouldn't want to talk about his life in Mexico and he could see no joy small-talking to a man who, as a Ranger, had tried his damnedest to string him up. Besides, he didn't feel like jawing; riding without a saddle was giving him hell. Though having a rubbed raw ass was his own fault. The old Mex had offered to swap horses with him, saying that he was used to riding without a saddle, but he had turned it down. Discomfort was better than showing weakness in front of the two Mexicans. Ritchie was beginning to find out his pride was growing.

They had caught up with Guereca where the main bunch of the raiders had split off from the herd to ride west towards the mountains. The cattle as they could plainly see, were still being driven southwards.

'Only six, seven men, with the cattle, Señor Langley,' Guereca said. 'Is that not so, Panchito?'

Panchito, hard *hombre*-faced, nodded.

Mart thin-smiled. 'Then the odds are in our favour, *amigos*. They'll not stand any chance facin' four feared *pistoleros*. If our luck still holds, we'll have drawn the first blood in our war against El Lobo.' Mart studied the lie of the land for a few minutes, wanting to keep luck riding with them, before he gave the orders to move out.

'Señor Guereca, and you, Panchito, stay in the open,' he said. 'Me and Ritchie will keep well back and low as before. Move along that big arroyo there, it seems to cut across the territory in the general direction the herd's headin''. And the same rule still stands, *señors*: any trouble you can't bluff your way out of, haul yourselves away from it fast. We won't be far behind you.'

Spurs jangling, Fiena walked towards the *cantina* with the pigeon-toed stride of a man who was more used to moving around on a horse than using his own two legs. He was bowed down with the weight of a bandolier of rifle reloads strung across his chest, two long-barrelled Colt pistols about his middle, and a heavy bladed knife swinging at his right hip. Plus the two bags of gold coins he had received in payment from Madero, the rancho who had bought the gringo cattle.

Madero hadn't haggled over the price for the herd so the deal had gone through quickly, allowing him and the five men with him to pay a visit to the village of San Ramon and enjoy a few bottles of tequila and the use of a woman – naturally both pleasures would be free: the feared name of El Lobo opened strongboxes, saw them fed, and made women easy to take, or painful death resulted.

Eight

It was the keener-sighted Panchito who first saw the horses tethered outside the *cantina* away to their left. He raised his right hand and gurgled a low warning cry. They kneed their mounts off the trail to take cover on the edge of a patch of chaparral.

Guereca had intended swinging clear of the village and keep following the trail of the herd. It would be foolish, he reasoned, to let their presence in the territory be known. An old man and a young boy, mounted on fine, saddled horses, would set village tongues talking. Loud enough, maybe, for El Lobo to hear and send men down from the mountains to find out how two ragged-assed *pacificos* came by their horses, and take them for himself, over their dead bodies.

Guereca's eyes hardened. The bloodletting, he thought, was coming earlier than the had expected. The horses could only belong to the men who had been with the herd. 'How many horses, Panchito?' he asked.

Panchito replied by raising six fingers.

Guereca wolf-smiled. '*Bueno*, then we have only six dogs to kill, not seven as we had thought. I will go into the village to see if I can find out when the *bandidos* are leaving, and try to stop them if they ride out before the two *señors* catch up with us. Once they are on the trail to the mountains we will have lost our chance of killing them.' Stopping them, Guereca knew, would mean taking part in a gunfight against odds he had no liking for. But after all, he thought, to cheer himself up, he wasn't expecting to kill them all, just hold them there until the *señors* came up. If he found a suitable hole in the ground and used his Winchester, he could shoot their horses, pinning them down in the *cantina*. If the hole he was going to make his stand in was close enough for him to see the horses, he thought sourly.

'You ride back to the *señors*, Panchito,' he said. 'Tell them to make haste to get here.'

Panchito shook his head vigorously, face twisted in a glaring-eyed scowl. He pointed at Guereca then thumped his chest, indicating to the old man that both of them should go into the village.

Guereca knew it made sense both of them going in. Panchito could move more swiftly,

64

had quicker reactions than he had. He was an old man, but the boy was no longer a boy and he had to stop thinking as though he was or Panchito would no longer look on him as his *amigo*. Panchito was an *hombre*, maybe only a small, skinny one, but one who had already killed twice. And there was really no need for him to ride back to Señor Langley to alert him that the *bandidos* were in the village. If it came to a gunfight then his gringo *compadres* would hear it and know they needed help, urgently.

'So be it, *amigo*,' he said. 'We go in on foot, our rifles hidden, backs bowed like broken-spirited *pacificos*, *comprende*?' Guereca grinned. 'If the *bandidos* see your face now, they will take you for an Apache warrior and lift your hair for the bounty they will get on it.'

The anger went swiftly out of Panchito's face. The old man had spoken true words. His *jefe*, Señor Langley, treated him as a real *hombre*, an equal; he didn't want to lose that respect by acting like a foolish boy. He drew out his rifle and swung down from his horse.

Fiena came out of the *cantina*, leaving the rest of his men still drinking and playing cards inside. He had a fire in his stomach

65

from the tequila he had downed, and a heat in his loins only a woman could cool. Unsteady-legged, he stumbled his way to the stream where he knew the women of the village would be washing their clothes. Only the older, dried-out women, he thought, sourly. The younger women of the village had gone into hiding on seeing his band ride in. He could force the village head man, on pain of being shot, to tell him where the virgins were, but even farmers, armed only with machetes and hoes, will fight back if pressed too hard. Some of his men could be hurt, or killed. And El Lobo would bury him up to his neck in an anthill for going into the village instead of returning to the stronghold, pronto, with the gold paid for the cattle.

Fiena stood at the water's edge looking at the woman closest to him, bending low with her skirt rucked up high to keep it out of the water. His eyes gleamed with lust as he took in the exposed plump, smooth thighs. Every now and again the woman, conscious of his gaze on her, stopped washing the clothes and glanced nervously over her shoulder at him.

Fiena's lips twisted in a cruel-eyed smirk. He liked his women to fear him. Then they would do his bidding without him having to waste his strength fighting to hold them down. Suddenly he caught a glimpse of movement in the brush on the opposite bank of the stream. His lecherous smile froze. It could have been a pig, or a village dog foraging through the undergrowth he thought. He drew out both his pistols and thumbed back the hammers. It could also be a villager suddenly finding his backbone, creeping in close with a knife in his hand to catch him off guard while he was having his pleasure with one of the women. Face a savage mask, he splashed his way across the shallow water shouting obscenities and firing his pistols into the heart of the brush.

Eva Marie flung herself to the ground screaming with terror as the pistol shells ripped through the brush just above her, showering her quivering body with splintered branches and leaves. She had been with the rest of the girls hiding in the crumbling adobe dwellings built by a long forgotten Indian tribe further along the stream. Older than the other girls, Eva Marie had felt bold enough to go back along the stream to see if the *bandidos* had left the village. Now she knew with fearful certainty they hadn't. Eyes shut tight, hands clamped over her ears, she gabbled frantic prayers to the Holy Mother to keep her from harm.

Fiena ceased firing as he stepped up to the brush. Warily, he pushed aside the thickets with the barrels of his pistols, ready to empty them of their remaining loads if he saw any more movement. Then he saw what he had never expected to see, the long, bare, slim legs of a young girl. His eyes widened with pleasure. Almost drooling at the mouth with hot-blooded anticipation, he slipped his guns back into their sheaths.

Slowly, Eva Marie opened her eyes and took her hands away from her ears. The shooting had stopped and her prayers had been answered: she hadn't been hurt. She began to inch herself up on to her knees and, with heart thumping wildly, began to crawl backwards out of the brush. She was almost in the clear when she felt hands grab roughly at her ankles. Eva Marie shrieked with terror as she was dragged bodily into the open, knees scraping painfully on the hard ground. She was flung over on to her back and found herself looking up at the leering, pock-marked face of a *bandido*. Eva Marie's scream reached an hysterical pitch as she tried to stand up and flee from her terrible fate.

Fiena struck Eva Marie a heavy, back-handed blow that brought tears of pain in her eyes and knocked her back to the ground, barely conscious. Then he was down on her, straddling her tightly with his knees, tearing at her clothes. Eva Marie, too weak to offer any more resistance against her attacker, lay there numb-brained, tears coursing down her cheeks, waiting for the terrible moment when she would be brutally deflowered.

Guereca cursed when he heard the shots and screams. He couldn't see who was doing the shooting or the screaming, but it meant that his plan of sneaking into the village unseen to find a spot where he and Panchito could cover the *cantina* with their rifles had fallen apart. At least one of the *bandidos* was out of the *cantina* and the others would be soon showing themselves to find out what the shooting and the screaming was about.

He turned to tell Panchito that they should go to ground and wait till things had quietened down, but the boy had gone from his side, racing off to the brush from where the screams had come. The *hombre* was in another of his killing moods. Guereca did some more cursing and followed him, praying that their gringo *compadres* weren't too far behind, for it seemed that Panchito could be leading them into the trouble Señor Langley had told them to steer clear of.

Silently, but fleetingly, Apache-like, Panchito slipped through the brush. The girl's screams had triggered off forgotten emotions in him. He was hearing again his own sister's screams as the Apache bucks used her. Then he had been too frightened to come to her aid. He had been too scared to help Señora Langley and her family. Now it was different, he was a bronco *hombre*, a wild one, who had killed and didn't fear death, and could help the girl who had screamed – if she wasn't now beyond helping. Though he could still kill the man, or men, who had made her scream.

Panchito's lips drew back in a fierce snarl when he came on to the *bandido* kneeling over the girl, kicking feebly beneath his bulky weight as he one-handedly loosened his pants. The good feeling that swept over Panchito realizing he was not too late, didn't soften the hardness of his face.

Fiena's manner of dying was fast and bloody. He sensed his danger and twisted his head round and saw the killing blade sweeping down. His eyes had only time to register a split second of frightened disbelief before his life gushed out of him in a hot, dark-red flood from the fearful wound in his neck. Contemptuously, Panchito kicked the sagging body off the girl and reached out a hand to help her to her feet.

Eva Marie, still half dazed from Fiena's blow, thought that the grim-faced boy standing alongside her with a blood-dripping machete in one hand a rifle in the other, was an Apache brave and his killing of the *bandido* had not been to rescue her but so he could take her for his own pleasure. Eva Marie sobbed bitterly as her fears reached new terrifying depths.

The 'Apache' smiled down at her, beckoning at her to stand. Suddenly he didn't seem to be a bloodthirsty Indian intent on ravishing her any more, and now he had been joined by an older man, a Mexican.

Limbs trembling, Eva Marie got to her feet, smiling weakly at her rescuer. Then, quickly lowered her head in blushing embarrassment, as she became aware she was showing a lot more of her body than it was right and proper for a young girl to be showing in front of men, complete strangers at that. Hurriedly, she clutched at her torn

71

dress, wrapping it round her in an attempt to cover up her exposed breasts.

Guereca noticed Panchito's goggle-eyed admiring look. He smiled inwardly. His life as an Apache slave hadn't turned the boy into a bitter-souled killer; he still held feelings of affection. Though he would soon be needing some of Panchito's killing lust. Peering through the brush, he had seen the rest of the *bandidos*, two of them the worse for drink, making their way to the stream. He was puzzled why they were not running, with their pistols fisted after hearing the shooting. Whatever, Guereca thought, this was no place for the young girl.

He smiled at the girl. 'You go, *señorita*,' he said. 'The *bandidos* are coming this way; they will want to do to you what that pig, Panchito sent to Hell, failed to do.'

'But what about you, *señor*?' Eve Marie asked Guereca, though her worried gaze was on Panchito. 'Are you not also in danger?'

'We are here to kill those *bandidos*, *señorita*,' Guereca replied, in a voice more confident than he was feeling. 'Now vamoose, pronto, before the killing starts.'

Eva smiled shyly at Panchito, wondering why he had not spoken. She stepped up close to Panchito and kissed him full on the lips, then ran back along the stream to the old dwellings.

Panchito had never been kissed by a girl before, and it was an experience he liked. If he'd had a tongue he would have yelled out his delight. He caught sight of old Guereca's worried look and his face steeled over, which pleased Guereca. The *hombre* was really only a boy with repressed youthful emotions and was entitled for some of them to show, but he didn't want him to stay as a boy, not when they had to face four *mal hombres*. If the young 'Apache' could kill with a rifle as well as he could with a machete then they had the chance of staying alive until their gringo *amigos* showed up.

The *bandidos* hadn't come fire-balling out of the *cantina* in alarm with rifles in their hands on hearing shots. They knew Fiena, when fired up with tequila, was loco enough to empty his pistol at anything that took his fancy. They had come down to the stream to grab a woman each before Fiena ordered them to ride back to the stronghold. Only there were no women here now, just piles of abandoned clothes. Fiena's wild shooting had sent them all running scared down-stream. And they could see no signs of

Fiena, who had ruined their chances of fooling around with the women.

'Let's get back to the *cantina, amigos,*' one of the *bandidos* said. 'We're wasting good drinking time trying to find the women, Fiena will be telling us it's time to ride out soon.'

Another *bandido*, gazing thoughtfully across the stream, smiled lewdly. 'That sonuvabitch, Fiena, will have kept a woman for himself. He'll be in the brush over there, having his way with her. We ought to cross and see if he wants any help to hold her down.'

Guereca waited until the raiders were close enough for Panchito, who had never fired a gun before, to have a fair chance of hitting one of them before drawing a bead on the man who had suggested crossing the stream. Feeling the long forgotten fear and excitement of once more taking part in a battle, albeit a small one, the old Juarista squeezed the trigger.

His target was flung backwards by the force of the close-range shot, dead before he landed in the water with a spray-raising splash, to leave a trailing red stain behind him from the gaping exit wound in his back as he floated downstream, arms and legs outstretched.

Panchito's shot was way off his target. The shell only kicking up a small waterspout well to the left of the man he had been aiming for. Groaning loudly at his disappointment, and with tears of pain from the sharp blow to his right cheek from the kick of his inexperienced holding of the Winchester blurring his vision, Panchito brought his rifle to bear again on one of the *bandidos*, and missed once more.

The firing became too hot for three of them and they ran back across the stream, firing wildly over their shoulders with their pistols. Guereca hit one of them in the leg that had him limping and cursing the last few yards before reaching the shelter of a dip in the ground. The fourth man, fisting two pistols, full of tequila-induced bravado, came on with a rush, firing his guns non-stop, and howling like an Apache.

He presented a target that Panchito, though flinching as the *bandido's* fire hissed frighteningly close above his head, couldn't miss. For one panicky moment he thought he had failed to hit him as the man still kept running towards him, though no longer howling. Panchito was about to take another shot at him when he noticed the raider's running had become a stumbling, leg-dragging movement and could clearly see the black-red oozing hole in his forehead and the lifeless-eyed face. Within feet of his rifle muzzle, the fast dying man stopped his running and fell to the ground as straight as a felled tree.

The *bandido* lay there, limbs jerking spasmodically. Panchito drew out his machete ready to deal him a killing blow when he heard his attacker give out a deep gasping sigh and his twitching stopped.

Guereca's congratulatory grin settled Panchito's taut nerves somewhat, but his hands were still shaking when he picked up his rifle to begin firing back at the *bandidos* holed-up across the stream.

Mart and Ritchie drew up their mounts on the outskirts of San Ramon, remaining hidden from any hostile eyes in the village, and took in the small war going on at the stream. Mart saw the muzzle flashes of two guns firing from the brush. The worrying ache in his belly eased. The old man and the boy were still alive.

He had heard the distant rattle of gunfire two miles back along the trail. 'Do you hear that, Langley?' Ritchie had said. Then, giving him a wintry grin, added, 'It sounds like our Mex *amigos* have run into trouble.'

Mart felt a tight ball of pain in the pit of his stomach. He didn't like anyone fighting his battles, especially a young boy and a man old enough to be his grandpappy.

'I heard,' he said, cold-voiced. 'And I reckon we'd better get our asses there fast. That's what *amigos*'re supposed to do, help each other out.' He dug his heels savagely into his horse's ribs. His mount, snorting angrily, took off in a back-leg kicking run, showering Ritchie with stones and dirt. Ritchie cursed, and rein-lashed his horse into a fast run to follow in Mart's trail dust.

Mart gave the village a sweeping, eagle-eyed look. 'Can you see any more of the bastards hangin' around, Ritchie?' he growled.

'If there are,' Ritchie replied, 'they'd be down at the crick pumpin' lead at our two boys for killin' at least one of their buddies. You can see one of the sonsuvbitches spread out just in front of where the old man and kid are pinned down. Now I calculate that if we go sneakin' in on foot behind those three characters doin' the shootin', we'll have them well and truly boxed in.'

'We ain't got the time for those tactics, Ritchie,' replied a thoughtful Mart. 'All the gunfire that's goin' on could draw some more of El Lobo's gang here soon. We want a quick end to the fightin'.' He smiled coldly at Ritchie. 'Me and you go in General Stonewall Jackson style, up on horses, hollerin' and shootin' every which way. That should kinda unnerve the bastards, put them off shootin' straight. But we leave one of them alive, the *hombre* furthest away from us, understand? I want him to take a message back to El Lobo.'

'Alive? Message?' said a surprised-looking Ritchie. 'What goddamned message would that be, Langley?'

'I'm takin' it that those assholes down there don't know they're bein' fired on by Mexicans so when they see two gringos comin' in cuttin' loose at them they'll think it's Texas Rangers who've jumped them. And that's what I want El Lobo to hear. If that murderin' sonuvabitch even suspects that Mexicans had a hand in gunnin' down his precious *muchachos* he'll come here and kill every livin' thing in this village, even the dogs. And I sure wouldn't want all those deaths on my conscience, Ritchie.'

Ritchie could understand the logic of the ex-Ranger's reasoning and surprisingly agreed with it. When he had found his boys dead and his cattle gone he hadn't given a damn if half the greasers in Chihuahua got killed if it got him within shooting range of El Lobo. Ritchie hoped he wasn't going soft. He should maybe start packing a Bible. He grinned at Mart.

'Let's do it your way, Mart,' he said. 'Promise me, though, if I get shot dead, don't put it around the border saloons that hard-man Ritchie got himself dead backin' up a coupla ragged-assed greasers will you?'

'I'll say you got killed protectin' women and girls from being raped and butchered,' Mart replied. He matched Ritchie's grin. 'Though if we both get downed, who the hell's goin' to get to know what happened here?' He drew out his pistol and thumbed back the hammer. 'Let's go and give those fellas a nasty surprise before the old man and the boy think we've ratted out on them.'

Guereca saw Mart and Ritchie's wild charge a few seconds before the *bandidos* realized that death was heading their way fast.

'Stop firing, Panchito!' he yelled. 'It's the gringos' turn to do the killing now!'

Sitting tall in their saddles, Mart and Ritchie bore down on the *bandidos*. Their hair-raising Rebel yell, a sound unheard this far below the border, froze the raiders' actions for several fatal moments. And as shells were beginning to kick up the dust around them, they came alive to their danger and made a break for it. Running for their horses tethered outside the *cantina*, firing wild shots in the general direction of the fast approaching gringos, it was a futile attempt to stave off their deaths.

Leaning sideways in their saddles, Mart and Ritchie gunned them down on the run with as much feeling as killing wolves. Ritchie drew a bead on the last *bandido* still on his feet, running along in a peculiar right-leg-swinging gait. He guessed that the man had already taken a shell in his hide from either the old man or the boy. And he owed the bastard one, he thought, for murdering his boys. He resisted the strong urge to put a killing shot between the shoulder blades, settling for a painful arm shot. The Mexican's howl of pain gave him some satisfaction.

Ritchie kept firing shots close to the running man until he saw him struggling on to one of the horses and high-tailing it out of the village pressed flat on its back. When Mart came up to him, he said, 'I reckon that fella really thinks his luck was in today, Langley.' He grinned. 'Bein' I'm a mean sonuvabitch, I plugged him in the arm, kinda lettin' him know how near he was in joinin' his buddies in Hell – and to prevent him from sneakin' back and usin' his rifle agin us if he still had any fight left in him.'

'The four of us have done a good day's work here, Ritchie,' Mart said, 'Six of El Lobo's cut-throats put out of action, five of them for good. We've drawn blood from the murderin' sonuvabitch, sooner than I expected.' He saw Guereca and Panchito come into view and make their way across the stream. 'And by the way the old man and the young *pistolero* are smilin' fit to bust, they must be unharmed. We're sure one helluva outfit, Ritchie.'

A pain-scowling Fabelo, hanging on to his saddle by the seat of his pants, cursed at his horse to make it go faster, to put as much distance between him and the Texan's deadly shooting. He cast a frightened-eyed glance behind him, and it eased his jagged nerves somewhat to see no sign of pursuit. He had escaped ending up as dead as his *compadres*, though Fabelo knew that death was still riding with him.

When he told El Lobo of the loss of his gold and the killings, death would only be a twitch of a trigger-finger away. If he hadn't been weakened by the loss of blood he would have ridden south, as far as Mexico City, out of reach of El Lobo's clutches.

Fabelo opined his only chance of staying alive was not to tell El Lobo they had been caught unawares in San Ramon but had been ambushed on the trail by a large band of Texas Rangers. His wounds, he thought, hopefully, should convince El Lobo how hard he had fought to stop the gringos from taking his gold. Fabelo's groans now weren't all caused by the pain of his wounds. The living that had bought his women and liquor for free, had now a due to pay, his life.

Nine

The villagers of San Ramon were crowded round the four *bandidos*-slayers. While they were pleased that several of the rapists and stealers of their meagre food stores, were dead, they were also fearful of the terrible revenge El Lobo would wreak on their village when he heard of the killing of his men.

Mart tried to reassure them that their fears were all for nothing. 'The *hombre* we allowed to escape,' he told them, 'did not see my two Mexican *amigos* so he'll report to El Lobo that it was Texas gringos who killed his *compadres*. We will take the *bandidos*' bodies and hang them from the nearest tree. A gringo punishment for murderers and cattle-thieves. Then El Lobo will have no doubts that a band of Texas Rangers is here in Chihuahua to hunt him down. You can take the *bandidos*' guns.' Mart smiled. 'M'be, when you feel the time has come, you will use the guns to kill some of the *bandidos* yourselves.'

The peons muttered amongst themselves, trying to get the measure of the four strangers. The long-faced gringo who had spoken so casually of hanging dead men was a man to be feared as an enemy, as was the other gringo with the cold-eyed look of a border *bandido*. Even their fellow country-man wearing a faded and ragged serape, old enough to have been a village elder's father, didn't look out of place riding with two gringo *pistoleros*.

The hawk-faced Mexican boy, sitting proud-backed on a fine horse, had the peons puzzled most. Yet he had proved himself an *hombre*, an equal with the two Texans, by killing with his machete the *bandido* who was about to ravish Gomez's daughter. He had the fierce look of the Apache.

Eva Marie's face was aching from holding her smile at her saviour, yet Panchito seemed to be deliberately ignoring her smiling glances. Her father had gone up to him, sitting there in his fine saddle, to thank him, but had only got a curt nod from Panchito in return. His coolness towards her puzzled Eva Marie. Wasn't she one of the prettiest virgins in San Ramon?

Panchito had noticed all the smiling he

was getting from the girl whom he knew now was called Eva Marie. He wondered, morosely, if she would sweet-smile at him if she found out he had no tongue and had been a slave of the Apache. And would Señor Gomez want his daughter to have a friendship with a dumb, ragged-assed, orphan boy? As hard as it would be he had to get all thoughts of friendship with Eva Marie out of his mind. His honour-bound duty to ride alongside Señor Langley, his *jefe*, in his mission to kill El Lobo, was all that should occupy his thoughts. Panchito's face took on a deeper hardness.

Mart had noticed the girl smiling and thought she was doing so with relief and happiness at her narrow escape from being raped by the *bandido*. Then he saw she was smiling at Panchito, but the Indian-visaged boy certainly wasn't basking in it. He gave Panchito a closer look and saw that the hardness wasn't showing in his eyes. 'Well, I'll be damned!' he muttered. Panchito held strong desires for the girl but he was too embarrassed and ashamed by his inability to speak to allow her to get close to him to find out for herself. Mart's feelings went out to him, as warm as if Panchito was of his own blood. He would have to try and give the boy's future some thought, if by riding with him he had a future, he thought, soberly.

'I am Gomez, the village headman, *señor*,' one of the men said to Mart. 'Your young *compadre* killed the pig who tried to *deflora* my daughter. I owe you a great debt. Although we are a poor village, *señor*, you and your brave *hombres* can take what supplies you need for the trail.'

'*Muchas gracias*, Señor Gomez,' replied Mart. 'Any supplies will be welcomed. Now to help yourselves; if El Lobo or any of his men come here to question you about the killings you say you saw four gringos ride past the village with some bodies slung across horses' backs. That oughta keep El Lobo thinking Texans are here in Chihuahua killin' his boys.'

After the villagers had left to gather up the supplies, Ritchie favoured Mart with an accusing look. 'You've showed that sonuvabitch, El Lobo, our hand, Langley,' he said. 'You should have told that Mex to tell them there was at least a dozen of us!'

'It wouldn't work, Ritchie,' replied Mart. 'El Lobo will have men with Injun blood in them, 'breeds who can read tracks clearer than me and you can read a newspaper. He'll soon cotton to the fact that there's only four of us. What we've just done is poke him in the eye with a stick. That'll make him kinda lose face, make him mad. Make him careless, I'm hopin', when he comes out of his hole-up seekin' us out, allowin' us to hit him again when and where we can. Cut down his *muchachos* so much that we can ride into his stronghold and finish him off for keeps. It ain't a great stick of a plan, I'll admit, and I'm open to offers of a better one.'

Ritchie's face screwed up thoughtfully for a minute or two, then he said, grudgingly, 'I guess stickin' our necks out is the only way. We sure can't surround him wherever he's forted up, even if we knew where the hell that was.'

Mart grinned. 'I was hopin' those dead fellas' horses will find it for us. If we turn them loose they'll head for where they know they're used to gettin' fed and watered. While we can't trail them right up to El Lobo's front door, because by then he'll have men out lookin' for us, they'll point us in the general direction of the stronghold without us risking our necks openly scoutin' the territory for tracks of big bunches of riders.'

'How the hell can we fail to plug El Lobo,

General,' Ritchie said, 'when we've got his horses workin' for us?' Ritchie's smile was genuine as he looked at Panchito. 'And the meanest *bandido* killer on both sides of the Rio Grande.'

Panchito felt six feet tall at the unexpected compliment from the Texas outlaw and he no longer disliked, or distrusted, Ritchie.

'Now let's go and get the offered supplies,' Mart said. 'Then we can ride out and find us some timber and have us a necktie party.'

Ten

Mart, face expressionless, looked up at the bodies swinging gently from the tree branches. He wished the men had been alive when the ropes had been put around their necks and hauled off the ground, so he could have told them of the personal reason for seeing them hang. Maybe, he thought, he would have the chance to slip a rawhide collar around El Lobo's neck and see him gasping and struggling for breath to prolong the last few seconds of his life.

Ritchie was feeling an uncomfortable tightness around his own collar. The stringing-up of Mexicans, *bandidos* or otherwise, didn't normally upset him. He had never put a noose around a man's neck before and this close to a hanging, even though the men were dead, had him thinking that he could have ended up dancing on air if he hadn't joined up with Langley on this crazy vendetta.

Not that he still couldn't end up dead, but it would be a cleaner, speedier death by the bullet, he hoped, and for a more honourable cause than stealing some rancher's cattle. Honourable? thought Ritchie, in surprise. That was a word that had never passed his lips before. Riding alongside an ex-Ranger was having an effect on him. He'd be quitting cattle-lifting when he got back to Texas, if he didn't quit living first.

They had put eight or nine miles between them and the grisly message left for El Lobo and had made their first camp on the trail. Though not expecting El Lobo's men to come hunting for them in the dark. Mart made it a cold camp, knowing that a camp-fire on the desert flats could be seen from great distances. Now, on the trail again, in the cool, clear early morning air, distinctive features of the mountains could be seen, the saw-tooth ridges, the sharp peaks and long-faced buttes. All eyes were alerted for signs of dust-clouds coming their way.

'I reckon it's time we gave our allies their heads,' Mart said. 'I can watch them from here with my army glasses until I get a sighting on what canyon they're makin' for.'

Encouraged by shouts and slaps on their flanks, the horses set off at a steady trot in a direct line for a twin-peaked mountain. Mart kept them under observation until he could only see the wisps of the trail dust.

Finally, he lowered the glasses and smiled at his *compadres*.

'They know where they'll find grain and water,' he said. 'They're still headin' for those two peaks; there must be an openin' to a canyon below them. We'll get in closer and wait for El Lobo to make his move and see if we can take advantage of it.'

'And I reckon we should get ourselves off these flats, Langley,' Ritchie growled. 'Someone with a pair of those fancy glasses could be sittin' up on one of those ridges gazin' at us. And we ain't forced to see the dust of any riders comin' out of those canyons; they could come sneakin' out and catch us by the balls when we're least expectin' them. The sonsuvbitches surprised my boys real good.'

Ritchie had a point, Mart opined. He must not let his hatred for El Lobo fault his judgement. Getting himself dead by being foolish wouldn't get him his revenge. Besides, he had three other lives to take into account; two only with him because of their loyalty to him.

'OK, Ritchie,' he said. 'We move along the washes and the gullies again. But someone will have to ride point, keep a looksee for any signs of El Lobo; we don't want to ride

91

blindly into any situation.' Mart knew it was an ideal job for Panchito and although he knew the boy would jump at the chance of once more proving himself an *hombre*, he hesitated to put Panchito into any more danger than he was right now.

Mart heard Panchito's gurgling efforts to talk and saw him gesturing at Guereca. Then Guereca said, 'Panchito wishes the honour of riding ahead of his *compadres*, Señor Langley.' The old Mexican smiled at Mart. 'Though the young *hombre* tells me it is wiser that he should scout ahead on foot.'

Whether or not the boy had understood what he and Ritchie had been discussing, or, like the Apache he had lived with, he knew what tactics were called for, didn't matter. It had saved him asking an awkward question. Though that didn't make him any happier accepting the boy's offer. To console himself, he thought that a man would need eyes as keen as a hawk's to spot Panchito moving around on foot in territory slashed by washes and gullies.

'Tell that young hellion, Señor Guereca,' he said, 'I will let him ride.' Mart smiled. '*Walk* point. But he's actin' as a scout not a one-man war party. He's not to take on any *bandido* with his knife or guns, *comprende*?

He comes back fast and reports to me if he sees any of El Lobo's men.'

'*Sí, señor,*' the old Mexican replied and began passing on Mart's orders to Panchito.

It was with mixed feelings that Mart watched Panchito speed along the bed of the wash, not raising a single spurt of dust in his passing as though he was running on air.

'The kid will be OK, Langley,' Ritchie said. 'He can move around faster and quieter than us old farts.'

Mart favoured the rustler with a quizzical glance. 'I thought you didn't care two hoots about greasers.'

Ritchie grinned. 'We could be headin' into one helluva gunfight, *amigo*, and there ain't many of us. I sure don't want one of them to be unfriendly towards me and not watch my back.'

'You needn't fret on that score, Ritchie,' Mart said. 'The kid's found his pride and when the goin' gets rough he won't let himself down by not playin' his full part in the action. Even if that means watching the back of a greaser-hating gringo cattle-thief. Now, let's move out and back the kid up.'

Panchito had hardly seemed to have left them when Ritchie called over his shoulder that the boy was coming back fast. 'And he ain't lookin' too happy. I reckon we should get ready for trouble.' He drew his rifle out of its boot and levered a shell into the chamber.

By the time the breathless Panchito reached them, the three, still mounted, were spread across the floor of the wash, rifles covering the bend in the wash beyond the running Panchito. Faces hard set, they were as ready as they could be to meet whatever trouble Panchito was haring back to tell them about. Panchito ran right up to Mart, leaning against his horse's flank to regain his breath before explaining to his *jefe* the reason for his early return.

'*Bandidos*?' Mart asked, sharply. Lowering his gaze on to Panchito long enough for him to see that he was no longer the stone-faced killer of *bandidos* but a frightened boy.

Panchito shook his head and pointed along the wash, then began walking back along the way he had come, indicating by waving his hands his *compadres* should follow him.

Mart shot Ritchie a what-the-hell? glance. The rustler shrugged. 'Whatever's along this wash has sure thrown a scare into the kid.' Then, as if some of Panchito's fear had rubbed off on him he brought up his rifle and nervous-eyed the rims of the arroyo.

As they rode through the dog-leg bend,

taut-nerved as prowling nocturnal tom-cats, Mart caught the acrid smell of a not so long dead fire, and another sickly sweet smell he couldn't place but was somehow raising the hairs at the nape of his neck. Clearing the bend they saw the wagon, or what the fire had left of it. The iron hoops that had supported the tarp cover stood out as stark as clean-picked buffalo ribs. The cover, all but a few scorched pieces, flapping in the breeze like a regiment's guidons, had been consumed by the flames. The body of the stout-built wagon was only a charred and smoke-blackened ruin.

The source of Panchito's fears and Mart's icy chills, lay crucified on one of the wagon's wheels. What had once been a man a few hours ago, was now a blackened, shrivelled mockery of a human being. He tasted the bitterness of bile at the back of his throat and saw Ritchie's face whiten with shock and horror and heard him cursing and dirty-mouthing. He opined the rustler was feeling the same way as he was.

Guereca crossed himself and muttered a hoarse, *'Madre de Dios!'* Panchito bit hard on his lower lip and clung tightly to Mart's stirrup.

'Apache?' Ritchie asked, as he dismounted.

95

'*Nada*,' replied Guereca. '*Yaqui*.'

'Who the hell are they?' Ritchie asked.

'They're first cousins to the Apache,' Mart said, almost snarling the words out, 'when it comes to inflicting pain on a man and still keeping him alive to suffer. Me and Guereca will go up on the rim to have a looksee. I reckon the red devils have finished their fun here and will be long gone, but if we don't want to end up roasted alive like that poor bastard there, it don't do to take things for granted.'

'Amen to that,' Ritchie said, fervently.

Before he set off to scramble up the bank, Mart said, in a lowered voice, 'Keep an eye on Panchito. I think the boy will be OK, but that ain't a sight even a grown man should ever cast his eyes on.'

Ritchie turned and looked at the drawn-faced Panchito and, reaching out, gripped his shoulder. He smiled in what he judged to be a fatherly manner, something his pa had never done to him. 'I reckon you're entitled to be more than a mite upset, Panchito,' he said. 'I fought in the big gringo war and I saw men killed all ways, but I'll tell you this, what I've just seen here almost made me throw up.' Ritchie sighed. 'I must be gettin' loco rabbitin' on like this, you

96

probably ain't understood a word I've been spoutin'. Now, let's look at the boxes that're lyin' about and see if they're holdin' anything that could be of use to us.'

By Ritchie's smile, soft-spoken words and friendly grip, Panchito knew the gringo *bandido* still thought of him as an *hombre*, still wanting him to ride alongside him as his *amigo* in spite of acting like a scared girl. The tension and fear eased out of his face.

Ritchie nudged Guereca in the ribs and pointed to the four arrow-spouting bodies lying a few yards away; they would be the rest of the wagon's escort, he thought, and the lucky ones – dead before they had been stripped naked and worked on with knives. Mart took another casting look across the flat, satisfying himself that there were no Yaqui skulking close by hoping to butcher some other unsuspecting traveller. 'OK, Guereca,' he said. 'Let's ride out, it ain't a joyful place to linger in.'

The wagon had been pushed into the arroyo, tipping over on to its side as it slid down the bank, spilling out its load of boxes and crates. Ritchie and Panchito were poking around the burst-open boxes when Mart and Guereca came slithering back down into the arroyo.

'There ain't any supplies, Langley,' Ritchie said. 'Just spades, picks, pinchbars and screws and bolts. I reckon the wagon was headin' for some mine in the mountains when the Yaqui jumped it.' He walked across to a small box that had been flung well clear of the wagon, its splintered top allowing some of its contents to spill out.

'Well I'll be damned!' Ritchie gasped. 'We could have something of use to us after all. Dynamite – a whole goddamned boxful! The Yaqui wouldn't know what it was; they couldn't eat it so they left it here. It's a pity they didn't try and light their fires with it. They would have entered their happy hunting grounds in bits and pieces.'

Mart walked over to him, eyeing the sticks of dynamite at his feet as though they were rattlers set to strike at his ankles. 'Is it safe to carry around?' he asked, dubiously.

'Of course it's safe,' replied Ritchie, grinning at Mart's obvious nervousness. 'It ain't "weepin'". Then it has to be handled real gentle. Now it's safe, unless you put a match to the fuses, six-second ones by the length of them.'

'How come you know so much about blastin' sticks, Ritchie?' Mart asked.

'Why, I ran a bank-heistin' gang before I

took up cattle-liftin',' replied Ritichie. 'And I've handled enough of the stuff to know it will give us a lot more edge than the guns we're totin'.' Which was a lie. In the one and only bank raid he had carried out, by using too much dynamite they had blown the bank, and half the town to pieces, without managing to force open the safe.

'OK, we'll take it with us,' Mart said, also seeing the advantage the dynamite could bring them. It could be their artillery. He gimlet-eyed Ritchie. 'But just see it's stowed away in our saddle-bags so that we don't save El Lobo the task of huntin' us down.'

The sticks were packed secure in their saddle-bags, excepting four sticks Ritchie stuffed in his coat pockets, just in case they rode into an ambush, he told Mart; it might give them the chance to cut and run for it. Mart would have liked to have seen the dead men buried but with Yaqui as well as El Lobo and his cut-throats ranging the territory they had to keep moving fast.

Mart wanted Panchito to scout ahead again, but thought the boy might not be up to it. He'd had a shock that would haunt most men until they passed over. Yet he needed his alertness to check out the trail ahead. The four of them could have gone blundering around the bend in the arroyo while the Yaqui were still having their pleasures at the wagon, and then they would have had one hell of a fight on their hands. He smiled encouragingly at Panchito. 'Are you ready to ride point, *compadre*?' he asked. Trying to sound as though what had happened in the wash was something not worth a second thought.

Panchito nodded his head; he was ready and eager to go. He had been hoping his *jefe* would still look on him as an *hombre*, forget how he had let him down by running scared. He turned to set off on his mission when he heard the gringo Ritchie call out his name. He paused and looked at him, wondering why the Texas *bandido* wanted to speak to him.

'Take these with you, Panchito,' Ritchie said, handing him two sticks of dynamite and several matches. 'Use them if you're in a tight corner, boy,' he said. Then he went through the whole mime of lighting the match on the butt of his pistol, applying it to the fuse then throwing the stick and crouching low, shielding himself with his arms to escape the force of the blast. 'Tell him, Guereca, he's only got six seconds before the big bang once he's lit the fuse.'

Panchito tucked the dynamite down the front of his shirt and slipped the matches into his pocket as he listened to Guereca explaining how little time he had to protect himself before the dynamite exploded. He grinned at Ritchie, signifying he knew how to handle the dynamite, then began running along the wash in ground-eating loping strides.

'I think the young sonuvabitch is lookin' forward to usin' that dynamite, gents,' he said.

'And that ain't a happy prospect at all, Ritchie,' Mart said. 'I don't want the kid to get a likin' for killin', and end up as a mean-eyed *pistolero*. Boot Hills on both sides of the Rio Grande are full of graves of young kids who fancied themselves as tough *hombres*. Panchito deserves a better future than that. And I've got the means to give him the chance to make his mark in life.'

He then told Ritchie of how Guereca had found two bags of gold coins on the body of the *bandido* who was attempting to rape the headman's daughter.

'I reckon it's payment for the cattle we were trailin',' Mart continued. 'So, by rights, it should be handed over to the Texas rancher you stole the cattle from, Ritchie.' He thin-smiled at the rustler. 'It sure don't belong to you. Me and Señor Guereca figure that the kid should have it. It will get him to a school of sorts where he can learn to write, whatever. And buy him a piece of land to work. It will give him a good start in life, providing we all make it through this business. The boy's got warm feelings towards that young *señorita* he rescued, and she's likewise towards him. Her pa might look more favourable on a dumb boy walkin' out with his daughter if he's a landowner.' Mart hard-eyed Ritchie. 'I take it you ain't opposed to the arrangement, *amigo*?'

Ritchie glanced over his shoulder. The old Mexican was also giving him a fish-eyed look. He was taking on the biggest killer in the whole of Chihuahua and could end up dead; trouble with his two '*amigos*' was something he didn't need. And to his surprise he agreed the kid should have the gold.

'You'll get no argument from me, Langley,' he said. 'The kid's proved himself worthy of it.' He grinned. 'And good *pistoleros* don't come cheap. Besides, if I had the gold, I'd only blow it all on whorin', drinkin' and gamblin' in some border ginmill. Now, if you've finished plannin' the kid's future, let's follow him. We don't want him to take on El Lobo and his wild boys on his own, do we?'

Eleven

Fabelo had spent a sleepless, painful night. Not even his regular pulls at the bottle of tequila was lifting his gloomy thoughts. On riding into the stronghold, more dead than alive, he had been told that El Lobo had retired for the night, along with a bottle of fine gringo whiskey and two young, virile girls. Though Fabelo wanted an end to his nerve-shredding uncertainty at what his *jefe's* reactions would be when he told him the bad news, disturbing El Lobo at such a delicate time would be asking for a bullet in the head, even if it had been good news he was carrying.

One of the women in the camp had dressed his wounds, but they still burned like the fires of hell. Fabelo rocked to and fro on his heels, moaning, and cursing the gringo Rangers, and Fiena for being such a horn dog as to seek his pleasures with a woman in San Ramon instead of riding here to the camp. And, more softly, he cursed El Lobo for making him sit here all night, cold and loose-bowelled with fear and pain while he was lying there warm and comfortable between two hot-blooded girls.

El Lobo came out of his hut, unsteady-legged, shirt-tails hanging loose over his pants. He paused for a moment, bleary-eyes squinting in the bright morning sunlight. He was in a good mood, still savouring the smooth warmth of his bed companions, who had performed to his expectations and the gringo whiskey still coursing through his veins. He caught sight of Fabelo. Gold teeth gleamed in the sunlight as he smiled. Hitching his pistol belt further on to his shoulders, he walked across to him in the slow careful steps of a man well liquored up.

'Ah Fabelo!' he said. 'You've brought the gold, eh?'

Then he noticed the look on Fabelo's face and the bloodstained bandages. Slowly, El Lobo's whiskey-fuddled brain grasped that his *muchacho* was about to spoil his good feelings. His welcoming smile slipped into a fiery-eyed glare, his good humour gone. 'There is no gold, Fabelo?' he hissed menacingly. 'Is there?'

'We were ambushed on the trail, *jefe*,' Fabelo said, the words rushing out. 'Texas Rangers, the rest of the *muchachos* are dead.

I fought back until I got these.' He pointed to his wounds.

El Lobo didn't give a damn about Fabelo's wounds, or his dead men – he could easily recruit others but being a taking man it hurt him deeply to have something taken from him. He didn't doubt that his men had been attacked by gringo lawmen. It was not the first time Texas Rangers had raided across the Rio Bravo. 'Was it a big troop of gringo pigs?' he asked.

Fabelo's hopes of living out his life rose. El Lobo hadn't, in a fit of his known wild temper, pulled out his gun on hearing of the loss of the gold and shot him; he was hearing him out.

'I don't know, *jefe*,' he lied, as confidently as he could. 'The shooting came that fast. M'be eight, ten rifles.'

El Lobo's lips tightened in anger. As well as being a killer and a thief he was also a born liar, and knew he was being lied to right now. The killing of his men hadn't happened as Fabelo had said. Had the gringo lawmen got the gold, or had Fabelo taken it from Fiena's body? He didn't think so; Fabelo wouldn't be so foolish to have taken the gold, but he was lying about something, and a man who couldn't be trusted was always a threat to him. He could betray him to the Federales for the bounty on his head, or harbour hopes of becoming *jefe*, whatever. His gold had gone and someone had to pay for its loss in blood for allowing that to happen just to ease his mind and to show that men who failed him were no longer his *muchachos*.

Fabelo saw his imminent death in El Lobo's mad-eyed look. Horrified, he backed away from him, arms raised in front of his body as though to ward off a blow from a fist. His screamed 'No! No!' was drowned by the noise of the rapid pistol shots that tore through his head.

El Lobo watched Fabelo's body hit the ground to lie there as a stark message to all in the stronghold that even here he lived up to his fierce name. The gringo lawmen who had stolen his gold, killed his *muchachos*, who didn't end up like Fabelo, would be the fortunate ones. Any captured alive were destined a few more painful hours of life, screaming it away buried up to their necks in an anthill, or dying just as painfully by the knife.

El Lobo fired the remaining loads in his pistol into the air to rouse the camp. There was killing to be done – even if he had to trail the gringo lawmen back across the big river.

Within half an hour of the execution of Fabelo, El Lobo, chivvying by curses and shouts, had his men in their saddles ready to ride out. Then he began to give his orders. This wasn't to be a raid on some village, or against an unsuspecting Texas cattle rancher where they could sweep in shooting and yelling, killing or frightening off all opposition against them; he had never clashed with the Texas Rangers before, but he knew of their reputation as hard-riding men who came in close, shooting fast and deadly, who feared neither *bandidos* nor bronco Indians.

'You, Tomas, you, Felipe, and you Jose,' he snapped, 'take four men each and scout four, five miles north and south. You are searching for eight to ten riders. A troop of Texas Rangers is here in our land. They have already killed Fiena and his men. The cowardly dog lying there fled rather than die alongside his *compadres*. Check on all the villages to find out if any of the workers in the fields have seen the gringos. I will be following behind you with another five *muchachos*,' El Lobo scowled fiercely at his three lieutenants – 'waiting with impatience for the news that you have picked up their trail.' His scowl changed into an even more fearsome smile. 'Try not to kill all of them; I want that pleasure. They will hear their screams clear across the Rio Bravo! Now pick your men and vamoose!'

El Lobo was the last of the band to leave the stronghold. He drew up his mount at the opening of a narrow, twisting defile that led out of the mountains. 'You *hombres* keep a sharp watch!' he shouted up at the two men perched on rocks on either side of the cleft. 'The gringos may be in Texas by now, or they may be sniffing their way through these mountains, so do not relax your vigilance. These Texas Rangers have fought the Comanche in their own land and fight and track like them.' El Lobo dug his spurs into his horse's ribs to catch up with his men, and to pass them when the trail allowed it. When it came to the spilling of the gringos' blood he wanted to be the first to dip his hands in it.

Twelve

Panchito had made it along the arroyo close enough to the foothills to see the large band of riders come into view from round the edge of a spur. His eyes glinted with excitement, and some fear. It seemed that the whole of El Lobo's raiders had come out of their stronghold to try and hunt them down. He began to count the number of riders using the fingers of both his hands, knowing that Señor Langley would want to know exactly how many *bandidos* they were going to fight.

Panchito knew it wouldn't be an easy fight, and he could be killed. For what chance, he reasoned, would he and his three *compadres* have against twenty-one fierce *bandidos*, even though Señor Langley and the gringo cattle-thief were hard *hombres*? If it was his fate to die before he was a day older he would gladly end it standing alongside his three *amigos* and maybe kill a few more *bandidos* before his time to die came.

Panchito saw the *bandidos* were splitting up into small groups of riders to ride across the flat until the furthest riders were only a distant dust haze. He grinned. Things didn't look so bad for him and his *compadres* after all. He could be soon killing. Four or five of El Lobo's men were only the same odds they had faced at the village. Panchito slid down to the bed of the wash to run back and tell Señor Langley of all that he had seen.

'We've drawn the bastard out, Ritchie,' Mart said, after Panchito, with much miming and frustrated grunts, had given him a picture of El Lobo's tactics. 'And they're spread out all over the territory. I reckon it's one of those chances we were hopin' would turn up. I figure we should be able to sneak by El Lobo's patrols and shove another stick in his eye, hitting him hard where it will hurt his pride most, in his own backyard. There can't be many of his boys left at the stronghold and they sure won't be expectin' an attack. If we do bump into one of the bunches of riders it should be no problem to shoot our way clear and go to ground in the mountains. What do you think, Ritchie?' Mart grinned. 'It'll give you the chance to show how expert you are with this dynamite we're haulin' around.'

Ritchie didn't think it was as good a chance as Langley was making out to dig El Lobo in the eye. He knew that sometime, if they lived long enough, they would have to make an attempt to destroy El Lobo's hole-up if they wanted to finish off the gang for good, but he felt right now wasn't the time, not with twenty odd killers out for their blood roaming around behind them. He was well acquainted with the saying, 'Between a rock and a hard place', but what Langley was proposing, he thought, was putting them between one hell of a lot of rocks.

He wasn't about to show his blowing cold on the mad-assed scheme, not when the bloodthirsty kid, by the look on his face, was itching to cut down some more *bandidos* with his machete again. Panchito, he felt, was beginning to respect him; he didn't want to lose that respect by the kid thinking he lacked the balls to fight. Though if he had faced the same odds in Texas he would have ridden sixty miles to avoid them.

He forced his face to show a 'What-the-hell' grin. 'You boys get me to that stronghold in one piece,' he said, 'and I'll blow it clear across the other side of those mountains, or my name ain't Joshua Ritchie.' He saw Guereca explaining to Panchito what he had been saying and the boy favoured him with a big open-faced smile and, in his tortuous way, speak back to the old man. Guereca's leathery face creased even further in a grin.

'The young *hombre* says you are a *bueno hombre*, Señor Ritchie,' Guereca said. 'He is proud to be your *compadre* and forgives you for being a gringo *bandido*.'

'Yeah, well, er,' Ritchie mumbled, wondering how a greaser kid's opinion of him mattered so much. His views on lots of things were changing, he thought. 'Tell him,' he said, 'I am also proud to be ridin' alongside an expert *bandido* slayer. Now, let's move out, Langley; havin' a bunch of El Lobo's boys snoopin' around behind us kinda unnerves me somewhat.'

Mart smiled. 'You oughta be used to havin' men comin' up behind you, Ritchie. I've chased you myself often enough.'

'It ain't the same at all,' growled Ritchie. 'You Rangers would have only shot me or strung me up, a quick clean death. What El Lobo will do to us if he takes us alive will be just as painful as what happened to that wagon's escort.'

With Ritchie's fearful prophecy ringing like the bells of hell in their ears, the four *compadres* pushed their horses along the arroyo towards the mountains, to face whatever trouble was waiting for them there.

Thirteen

Jose crossed himself and his face lost some of its colour as he looked up at the wind-swinging bodies of Fiena and his *compadres*. Cursing, he ordered the bodies to be cut down. His band had pulled off the main trail, guns fisted, to check on the movement he had glimpsed in the trees, only to find it was caused by dead men, *compadres*, not by the gringos they were searching for. Jose's cursing became more profane when it was discovered that the men had been shot dead before they were roped by the neck to the branches of the trees. No death, he thought angrily, could be too painful for the gringos when they were caught.

Now he had the unenviable task of telling his *jefe* the manner of his *muchachos'* deaths. He hadn't expected to find the gold payment for the cattle on Fiena's body, but he had all the dead men searched before sliding them into the shallow burial pit they hacked out of the hard ground with their machetes. 'Did you find my gold?' would be one of the first questions El Lobo would put to him, if he didn't shoot him dead on hearing the fate of Fiena and his band.

The cry, 'There's only tracks of four horses with riders on!' from one of his men had Jose puzzled for a moment or two. El Lobo had spoken of as many as ten Texans ranging the territory. A closer reading of the tracks couldn't determine whether or not the gringos had ridden north to the border, or were still here in Chihuahua. Jose shrugged. He would let El Lobo figure out who the gringos were who hanged dead men.

A stone-faced El Lobo listened to Jose's report of the finding of the bodies and, wanting to get all the bad news out at once, also told his *jefe* that the gold was gone. Then he waited, nerves and teeth gritted for El Lobo's show of temper that would have him yanking his pistols and shooting him dead. To his relief, all he got was a narrow-eyed suspicious glare from him.

'Are you sure about the gold?' El Lobo growled.

'*Si, mi jefe!*' Jose replied. 'The gringo dogs must have taken it. And, there were only four of them. We tried to track them to see if they were on their way back to the border, but they had covered their trail.'

El Lobo's eyes widened as surprise replaced suspicion in his mind. He flicked his quirt against his right leg as he began to think just who the gringos were who had killed his boys and stolen his gold. He cursed Fabelo's soul, hoping that it would rot in hell. He had suspected that Fabelo had lied to him about being ambushed on the trail by a band of Texas Rangers. If that had been so why hadn't there been any bloodstains on the saddles of the dead men's horses when they came back to the stronghold? There wasn't even a scratch on their hides and they had been in the middle of a gunfight. But his mind, occupied with meeting a threat of an attack by Texas Rangers, hadn't registered that fact then.

No, El Lobo thought, the four men could only be cattlemen, or hired *pistoleros*, who had tracked the cattle and waited until Fiena had made camp and caught them unawares. The hanging of the dead men was intended as a warning to any Mexican who stole gringo cattle, of what their fate would be, alive or dead.

Suddenly El Lobo stayed his quirt-wielding hand. He was getting an uneasy feeling that he had been meant to read things that way. Why hadn't the Texans taken the horses, he wondered? They wouldn't leave six horses and their saddles, worth good money in Texas, without some reason? And why had they hidden their tracks if they were riding for the border?

It could only mean one thing: whoever they were, their business in Chihuahua hadn't ended with the killing of six of his men. The gringo sons-of-bitches were still here and he and his men were their targets. El Lobo stood up in his stirrups and looked about him as if he could see the mysterious riders.

'You gringo dogs!' he yelled, face a mask of anger and hate. 'You have killed your last Mexican. You will never see the Rio Bravo again!' He dropped back heavily on to his saddle and glared mad-eyed at Jose.

Jose shivered. He had never seen his *jefe* so loco before; he could still die within the next few seconds.

'Jose,' El Lobo barked, 'take your band and three of my men and look for sign of those four gringos. I do not think they have left Chihuahua. They let the dead *much-achos'* horses go so they could track them to our camp. I do not think they're foolish

118

enough to attack our stronghold, bu[t] could have seen us ride out and split up i[n] small bands and be lying in wait to ambush us as they must have done with Fiena.'

El Lobo leaned forward in his saddle, the madness still in his eyes. 'Search well, *amigo*, because I want to finish their killing here painfully and for good. I will pick up the rest of the *muchachos* and check on every village between here and the border. Some villager must have seen them pass. There could be more of the dogs.' El Lobo's grin in no way softened the savageness of his look. 'No villager dare lie to El Lobo. And remember, Jose, I want the gringos alive, *comprende*?'

Jose gave out a dry-throated, '*Si, jefe*,' fully understanding that if he didn't bring the gringos in alive he had written out his own death warrant.

they
nto

Fourteen

The trail snaked its way through the foot of the mountains, parts of it almost closed in by beetling bluffs, until it was only wide enough for three horsemen to ride abreast. Ritchie had to admit that trailing the dead *bandidos'* horses had been a good idea of Langley's. Without them giving a pointer in which direction El Lobo's camp lay, Panchito would never have seen the *bandidos* ride out. They could have spent days searching every canyon, every cleft for the true trail, with all the danger that would have heaped on them.

He was bringing up the rear, and kept glancing nervously behind him, ears finely tuned for the ominous sounds of the chinking of horses' hooves on stones on their back trail. And he had a lit cheroot in his mouth, ready to spark off the fuse of a stick of dynamite if his fears became a reality.

Ritchie figured that a single stick would down a fair section of the rock face on both sides of this tunnel of a trail, effectively cutting off any pursuers, and their own way out, other than riding wild-assed through an alerted hostile camp in the hope of finding some exit out of the mountains on the far side. Or leaving their horses and tackling the high ridges on foot before they died of thirst. What the hell, Ritchie thought, philosophically; when he had crossed the Rio Grande he knew he wasn't embarking on a picnic ride.

Mart raised his right hand to bring his small column to a halt when Panchito, acting as point again, came running back to him; a worried looking Panchito pointed to the left side of the pass then to the right side.

'Guards, Panchito, two of them?' He raised two of his fingers. Panchito nodded. 'Show me,' Mart said and drew out his rifle and dismounted and walked behind Panchito to the next twist in the trail.

The guards were squatting on flat-topped pillars of rock facing each other, looking like two great birds of prey wrapped in their dark-coloured serapes. Easy targets for the Winchester, Mart thought, though gunfire would lose them their only edge, surprise. His tactics were to hit the camp hard and fast with guns and Ritchie's dynamite, then pull out quickly before the *bandidos* knew what the hell had hit them.

The guards would have to be disposed of silently. Close-quarter knife or machete work, getting near to them without being spotted and the alarm raised didn't seem possible. Lady Luck had brought them this far all in one piece; she wouldn't clear the way to the camp for them. It was time, Mart thought, he discussed tactics with Ritchie and old Guereca. Mart smiled inwardly and, of course, the young *pistolero*, Panchito.

'Any idea how we can get by them, Ritchie?' Mart said, after he had explained the problem to the rustler and old Guereca.

'All I know, Langley,' replied Ritchie, 'is that if we can't remove those two bastards without them raisin' the alarm but fast, I reckon we should get the hell outa this deathtrap of a pass, just as quickly and pick another day to poke a stick in El Lobo's eyes. I've been in some tight corners before – you've put me in two or three tight spots – but if that bunch of *bandidos* Panchito saw ride back along this trail then, *amigo*, we're sure in one tight corner, one we ain't likely to get out of alive.'

'Yeah, I know that!' Mart said sharply, feeling frustrated at getting this close to dealing El Lobo a crippling blow only to find that time was running out on him. 'I'm workin' on it, but I ain't no army general.'

'Maybe I and Panchito could remove those guards silently, Señor Langley,' Guereca said.

'I'm all ears, *compadre*,' replied Mart, his hopes rising knowing that the old Mexican wasn't a blowhard. 'The two of us...' Guereca began, and told Mart and Ritchie of his plan.

'It could work, Langley,' Ritchie said, when Guereca had finished speaking. 'Unless you can come up with a better plan.'

'Yeah, they could pull it off,' replied Mart. 'But it's puttin' the boy at risk again.'

'Jesus H. Christ!' Ritchie gasped. 'The kid at risk? Ain't he had his life on the line since we set off on this hunt? We're damn well sittin' here up to our eyeballs in *risks* knowing what's ahead of us and what could soon be comin' along the trail behind us. And look at the way the boy is grinning. The young hellion's all for Guereca's scheme. And, as the old man said, what threat would the guards see in an old man and a boy?'

Mart knew Ritchie was right. He had to stop thinking of Panchito as a boy. He had more than proved himself an equal and wanted to be treated like one with no special favours. The boy had great need to pay off a debt of honour he felt he owed him and that was something he had to respect. He grinned at Guereca. 'You do it, old man,' he said. 'And good luck to you both.'

The sounds of ribald singing echoing up from the defile had both guards springing on to their feet, rifles held ready. They exchanged puzzled glances which quickly turned to grins as they saw the old man, leaning heavily on the shoulders of a boy, come into view. Every now and then the old man's legs would fold up beneath him and the boy would have to grab him to keep him from falling down, all the while the old drunk keeping up his out-of-tune singing of a popular lewd love song.

'Hey, Carlos!' one of the guards shouted across to his *compadre*. 'Let's go down and find out if that drunken old goat dances as well as he can sing, with a little help from this!' He tapped the butt of the big pistol sheathed on his right hip. 'After we ask him how he came by this trail!'

'The dogs are coming down, Panchito!' Guereca whispered. 'Look scared, and don't swing your machete until I give the sign. If the camp is alerted, all the killings we have done so far will have been in vain. El Lobo will still be alive to kill and rape in Chihuahua, while we and our gringo *compadres* will be dead.'

'*Buenos dias, amigos!*' Guereca said, favouring the guards with a drunk's loose-faced grin as they came along the trail, grinning at the fun they were about to have making the old man leap around to avoid getting a bullet in his feet. In a tangle-footed walk, Guereca, dragging Panchito along with him, got within touching distance of the *bandidos*, praying that they had been fooled enough not to notice that they couldn't smell the strong fumes of tequila wafting off a man who was rolling drunk.

Mart covered them with his Winchester, ready to gun down the guards if they saw through Guereca's dangerous play-acting. He was discovering that the lives of his *amigos*, especially Panchito's, were more important to him than getting revenge for the killing of his wife.

Guereca, still showing his inane grin, squeezed Panchito's shoulder, the signal that the killing time was here. Then his hand slipped down to the long-bladed knife stuck in the top of his right boot.

Panchito made his move. Giving out a

gurgling, triumphant cry he brought his hand gripping the machete up from beneath his serape. Before the guard could take in his danger in the changed look on Panchito's face, the machete slashed across his neck in a vicious back-handed sweeping blow. Panchito's hand poised in mid air, ready to bring the blade down for another fearful cut if it was needed. Then as he saw the growing crimson collar spreading around the man's neck and unnatural droop of his head, he knew it would be a wasted blow. He didn't wait to see the already dead man fall to the ground but whirled round to see if his *compadre* needed help.

As old as he was, Guereca had done his killing, not so messily as Panchito's, but just as quickly and silently. Like Panchito's *hombre* his man was also caught off guard. The thin blade was up to its hilt in the *bandido's* chest before it showed in his face that he was being stabbed, Guereca stepped in close and put his free hand over the dying man's mouth to stifle his cries from the blinding flash of pain he felt as his heart burst. Guereca held him in a tight embrace as though he was greeting a long lost brother until the full dead weight of a corpse was draped over his shoulders.

Guereca pushed the body away from him to let it drop to the ground, unsteady on his legs as a real drunk. It had been a long, long time since he had killed a man with cold steel. And the man he had shot at San Ramon was the first he had killed with a rifle since his days as a Juarista. He was about to get the feel of it again now the way to El Lobo's encampment had been cleared.

Guereca glanced at Panchito's kill, as bloody-looking as if it had been a body lying on some battlefield. When the boy killed, he really killed. A bloodthirsty trait he must have picked up from the Apache, he opined. 'Bueno, amigo,' he said, then gave a tight grimace of a smile. 'Now we are about to pay the debt we owe to Señor Langley, Panchito.'

Mart gave a sigh of relief and lowered his rifle. The pair had pulled it off, their luck was still riding high. Now Judgement Day had come for those sons-of-bitches up ahead. He stood up and waved for Ritchie to bring up the horses. He grinned as the ex-rustler came closer. The dynamite 'expert' was about to set up in business again, he had a lit cheroot in his mouth.

They were all mounted up and Mart issued his brief battle orders.

'Ritchie, you and Panchito can handle the dynamite,' he said. He knew the boy could kill with his machete better than most men, but he may not be so efficient sending *bandidos* winging their way to Hell wielding a heavy long gun. 'Tell him to use the first stick to spook the horses.' Mart hard-eyed Ritchie. 'Spook them, not scatter them in little pieces across the high ridges. Then blow up their huts, tents, whatever, and any supply wagons you see. Keep the bastards runnin' around in a panic so they make a stand against us.'

'OK, *mi Generale*,' replied Ritchie. He grinned. 'Do you figure the kid's old enough to smoke one of these?' Ritchie drew on the cheroot and blew out a cloud of strong-smelling smoke.

'The boy's picked up some bad habits since he trailed with us, Ritchie,' Mart said, hard-voiced. 'Smokin', I reckon, will cause him no problem. And there's one other thing: there'll be women and kids in the camp, take care not to hurt them when you're throwin' your dynamite around.'

'M'be your boys, Langley?' Ritchie said.

Mart shook his head and, not meeting Ritchie's gaze, said, 'I don't think so, Ritchie.' He sat silent in his saddle for a

129

moment or two, thinking of how things might have been for his family if he had been there when El Lobo raided the village. The only difference, he thought bitterly he would have been dead alongside his wife and there would be no one to avenge their deaths. He looked directly at Ritchie. 'Let's go and make sure that the same fate don't happen to any more children in Chihuahua.'

Just past where the dead guards' look-out posts had been, the trail ended and a bluff-enclosed grassy basin opened up before them. Shacks and tents were dotted along both sides of a stream that ran through the basin. Mart could see two wagons with tarp covers over their load, prime targets for his dynamiters. What men were in sight – Mart estimated ten or twelve – were squatting at fires, talking and drinking, unaware, he noted with grim satisfaction, of the big trouble about to hit them. The women were at the stream doing their chores while their children played in the water. They would be well out of the action when it began.

He pointed to the horse lines at the edge of a small stand of timber just ahead of them; Ritchie gave him the thumbs up sign, then he gave the order to dismount, tying up their horses in a patch of brush that hid them from the men at the fires. 'Tie 'em tight,' he said. 'We don't want them to take off as well. We want to leave the hell we're gonna raise here fast!'

Mart took a final look at his *compadres* he could be leading to their deaths, before he gave the signal for the hell he was about to create to begin. They were as grim-faced as he was, contemplating the odds they were about to take on. Even Panchito, with a smouldering cheroot stuck in the corner of his mouth, seemed to have aged ten years. Though he couldn't see signs in any of them of the weakening of the resolve to carry out what they had vowed to do, namely the killing of El Lobo. Mart's lips twitched in a faint smile. They were a bunch of god-damned Daniels about to enter one hell of a lions' den. He gave Ritchie a curt 'Now' nod.

Ritchie's grin was as thin as his. He was trying not to dwell too long on the dis-comforting thought that if he and the kid were shot above the knees they need not worry about how they would get the wound seen to. With all the dynamite they had stuffed in their pockets and down the front of their shirts, they would both disappear from the face of the earth in one God almighty bang.

Bold-faced, for Panchito's sake, he said, 'Tell the boy, Señor Guereca, he can have the honour of openin' the ball by skedaddlin' the horses.'

Almost before the old man had finished speaking, Panchito was drawing hard on his cheroot until it glowed red at the tip. He hoped that the foul smoke would not cause him to have a coughing fit and he would let down his *compadres* by not being able to throw the dynamite. Fighting to stay calm, he touched the fuse against the end of his cheroot, watched the spluttering flame take hold, then stepped clear of the brush to have an unhindered throw.

The stick cut a flaming arc in the air, landing where he had aimed for, just yards short of the horse lines. Ritchie's stick trailed his, bouncing in the middle of the nearest group of men at one of the fires. Both explosions came simultaneously. The noise – and its fearful aftermath – held Panchito, who had never witnessed dynamite exploding before, spellbound with shock and amazement.

Through the split-second orange flash and the column of dirt and stones raised by Ritchie's stick, he saw the blurred shapes of bodies, arms out-flung, fly backwards through the air. He heard the high-pitched shrieks of badly wounded men and the squealing of terrified horses, and glimpsed through the settling dust of his own stick, the horses splashing their frantic way across the stream, trampling down women and children in their mad dash for safety.

Ritchie gave him a smile and began to move forward, his arm held back, set to throw another stick. Panchito got over his shock and grinned back at him and then walked alongside his gringo *compadre*, seeking another target. The men at the other fires scattered for cover from the sudden, noisy death that was raining down on them, thinking at first they were being attacked by Federale troops armed with cannons. Mart and Guereca, coming up behind the dyna-miters, cut loose at the fleeing *bandidos*, bringing two of them tumbling down.

They worked their way through the camp, slowly and methodically, destroying every building in the way, meeting any resistance with dynamite or rifle fire. Panchito hurled a stick at a hut from where they had been fired on. The hut was blown apart and the firing ceased.

A sudden burst of gunfire from the far side

of one of the tarp-covered wagons had the four of them grabbing for the dirt as shells hissed close by them.

'Can you get the sonsuvbitches, Ritchie?' Mart shouted. 'We can't pick them off with our rifles!'

Ritchie raised his head slightly and judged the distance. He reckoned he could just about reach the riflemen with a stick if he stood up and got a good arm swing at it. He also judged if he got to his feet he would get himself dead before he had the chance of making the throw.

'Naw!' he yelled back. 'Not from this position, eatin' dirt. And if me and the kid so much as raise ourselves on to our knees we'll get our heads blowed off!'

Mart did some rapid thinking. Speedy and destructive had been the essence of their attack; to kill as many of the *bandidos* as they could and have the rest running scared across the mountains. Time for a pitched battle was something they hadn't got. Some of the main band of El Lobo's men could have heard dynamite going off and could be haring back to the camp. Running short of dynamite and rifle loads they would have lost all the edge they had started the raid with and El Lobo would have the last laugh,

134

seeing them buried on some anthill.

Somehow, Mart thought, the men who had them pinned down had to be distracted, long enough for him to cut away to his left. The ground dipped sharply there and could give him the cover to work his way round the wagon and come at them from behind. That is if he could make the thirty-second dash to the dip without getting gunned down. The tarp-shrouded wagon going sky high, he reasoned, could put the riflemen off long enough for him to clear the open ground unharmed.

'Can you blow up the wagon there, Ritchie?' he called out. 'It'll give me the chance to get at those sonsuvbitches!'

Ritchie risked an assaying look at the wagon. It wouldn't be as long a throw as where the riflemen were, but he would still have to stand up to heave the stick, an impossible to miss target for them. He was aware as much as Mart was that the longer they stayed here the greater the danger of being trapped in the camp by El Lobo. Risks had to be taken if they wanted to be able to ride out of the mountains alive.

'Give me a coupla minutes, Langley!' he answered. 'And I'll see you're screened from those riflemen real good!'

He gave Panchito a stern-faced look and pressed him closer to the ground. He had no doubts that if the kid knew what he and Langley had been discussing he would have ignored the rifle fire and got to this feet and maybe run closer to the wagon before throwing the dynamite. Then Langley would have bawled him out for getting the kid killed. He raised a warning finger. 'Stay put, Panchito,' he told him. 'I've got to help out Señor Langley.'

Ritchie, with his belly tight to the ground, angled away to his left to put more of the bulk of the wagon between him and the riflemen. He had sidled, crab-like, four or five yards when he noticed the spurts of dust raised by the rifle shells were well away from him. He could risk standing up. 'Get ready, Langley!' he shouted, and touched off the fuses of the sticks of dynamite he held in both hands. In one quick movement Ritchie leapt to his feet, threw the sticks, and dropped back to the ground again. The twin explosions sounded like rifle shot to the shattering noise that followed.

With an eye-blinding flash, and a bang that shook the earth beneath the four *compadres*, the wagon blew apart. Only their nearness to the explosion saved them from serious injury or death from the flaming pieces of shattered, burning timber that swept over them with the destructive force of a gigantic charge of cannister shot.

Mart, halfway to his feet, to start his mad-ass dash, was knocked down by the blast, and stayed down, flinching and cursing as hot splinters of wood burned his hands. He reckoned he was lucky not to be sailing sky-wards with the wagon.

Back to being a boy again, a fearful Panchito, to escape the fiery rain, pressed his face so close to the ground he had difficulty in breathing. A dazed-faced Ritchie was the first to stand up and gaze on his handiwork. Where the wagon had been was now only a crater strewn with blackened, smoking timber. He grinned, weakly. Langley wanted a distraction, he couldn't have given him a bigger one without blowing the whole camp sky high.

Mart wasted no more time, he set off running for the dip and his delayed out-flanking manoeuvre against the riflemen. Then Guereca and Panchito came alive. Shaking the dust and smouldering debris from their clothes, they walked warily round what had been the wagon, rifles held across their waists to back up Mart. Ritchie came round from the other side of the crater to join them.

They met Mart coming back. 'They're dead,' he said. 'At least two of them are; one of the wagon wheels landed slap bang on them. The other fella's took off.' He looked around the now-deserted encampment and could only hear the low moans and groans of wounded men. 'There don't seem anyone left who's itchin' to make a fight of it.' He smiled thinly at Ritchie. 'That was one hulluva bang you set off. The wagon must have been loaded with powder for El Lobo to make his reloads with.'

Ritchie grinned. 'It did the job, didn't it?'

'Yeah, it did that,' replied Mart. 'And it's time we were pullin' outa here. That bang must have been heard in Presido. Panchito, bring up the horses, you, Ritchie, check that other wagon for supplies, then blow it up. Me and the *señor* will gather up some reloads for our guns. We've got five minutes, that's all.'

Mart cast one last over-the-shoulder look at the devastation they had caused in the camp. He gave a satisfied grunt. Hell had sure been raised. Whatever other grief they may inflict on El Lobo, the destruction of his camp meant that he and his men and the women and children had a cold, hard winter coming to them. Mart was beginning to taste the sweetness of revenge.

As they rode through the narrowest part of the pass, Ritchie called on them to halt. 'Let's finish the job off!' he said. 'Close the bastard's front door for good.' He stood up on his saddle and jammed a stick of dynamite in a crack in the rock face. Thumbing a match into flame, he lit the fuse then dropped down into his saddle. 'OK, *amigos*, get ridin' before the whole goddamned mountain comes tumblin' down on us!'

The *amigos* didn't need spurring on, they had seen the damage a stick of dynamite could do. Heels were dug into horses' ribs and they raced out of the pass, heading for the shelter of the big arroyo, to hole-up someplace and lie in wait for another chance to strike at El Lobo. Behind them, they heard the sounds of rocks crashing down, blocking for ever El Lobo's main trail into what was left of his stronghold.

Fifteen

Jose thought he had heard the distant rumbles of explosions in the mountains, but he could see the dark thunderheads swirling around the high ridges and thought no more about them.

He and his band had come across the burnt-out supply wagon and the mutilated bodies, and were now following the tracks of four horses clearly seen on the bed of the arroyo. Jose gave a smile; they could only have been made by the mounts of the men they were hunting. His smile became a derisive sneer when he saw the trail was leading them towards the mountain pass to their stronghold. They must be loco, he thought, thinking that the four of them could attack their camp. Between him and his men and those in the camp, the fool-hardy Texans were as good as taken.

Then Jose heard another bang that rattled around the mountains, removing the cocky smile from his face, and knew the earlier noises hadn't been thunder. In a moment of confused panic, he thought the gringos were attacking the camp with cannon. Thinking more lucidly, he asked himself how it could be possible for four men to haul a heavy cannon into the mountains, and they hadn't seen any wheel ruts on the trail. It could only be dynamite the Texans were using. The Texans weren't mad after all.

Another bang, much nearer this time, brought the smile back on to his face again. The gringos were coming out of the mountains. Whether they had been driven out, or had done what they had intended to do didn't matter, he would find out when he captured them.

'Ride fast to El Lobo!' he ordered one of his men. 'Tell him we have the Texan dogs!' He looked up at the high sides of the arroyo then grinned icily at the rest of his band. 'The gringos will ride back this way, thinking themselves safe; we shall be waiting for them, back there.' He pointed over his shoulder to where the arroyo bent sharply. 'We will trap them here where the banks are too steep for their horses to climb.' Jose's face hardened. 'Remember, *amigos*, El Lobo wants them taken alive, or we will be lying dead alongside them.'

Ritchie was riding slightly ahead of his

compadres glancing nervously at the scrub-covered sides of the arroyo. He could see nothing to alarm him, but something was causing his uneasy ass-shifting in his saddle. A man who had lived on the wrong side of the law all his adult life developed a trait for smelling trouble before it hit him between the eyes, or he didn't stay an owlhoot long.

He picked out the hoof marks of their horses made on their way to the stronghold clear enough, then Ritchie's eyes narrowed, at the fresh tracks of several horses that turned and led back along the arroyo. His uneasiness had been for a reason. He drew out his rifle from its boot and cradled it in his arms, his gaze all the while checking out every rock, every patch of brush for the giveaway glint of a gun. He pulled his horse to a halt. Mart drew up alongside him, and gave him a questioning look.

'A piece up ahead,' he said, softly, 'is an ambush party sittin' there waitin' for us.'

Mart stiffened in his saddle, not doubting Ritchie's reasoning. Their luck had to change for the worst sometime.

'We ain't dead yet, Ritchie,' he said, in a voice as unyielding as his look. 'Not without a fight.'

Ritchie laughed derisively. 'That's "glory-

143

boy", talk, Langley! I had a bellyful of that kinda hogwash durin' the war. You ain't leadin' a bunch of wild-assed Rangers, you're gonna charge head-long into an ambush with an old man and a kid!'

'What do you reckon we should do then?' Mart snapped. 'Hold up our hands and beg El Lobo for mercy?'

'No, I don't!' replied Ritchie. He grinned at the angry-faced Mart and tapped his pocket. 'I didn't use all the dynamite at the stronghold; these are my aces in the hole and it looks as though it's time I played a card or two. While I'm keepin' those sonsuvbitches' heads down, you and our two *amigos* hightail it outa this death trap and head back to the mountains. I opine in the confusion two sticks of dynamite will cause among those fellas, it should allow me to swing round them and catch up with you.'

Mart closed-eyed Ritchie. 'And you're the *hombre* who don't believe in "glory-boy" tactics.'

'Whatever it is, Langley,' Ritchie said. 'It's the only chance of us gettin' out of this situation alive. We could try and sneak back the way we've come, but the bastards could be howlin' for our blood before we got a coupla hundred yards. And even if we did make it to the flats, how long do you think old Guereca and the kid can stay up on their horses in a hell-for-leather chase?'

As much as Mart disliked splitting up his small band, Ritchie's plan made sense. It was a chance to keep them alive, leastways three of them, he thought, soberly, to carry on the fight against El Lobo. Ritchie was taking one hell of a gamble with his ace-in-the-hole cards.

'OK,' he said. 'You go and sow your confusion, but don't be so bold-assed as to try and make a fight of it. Get out fast. We'll head for the stronghold pass and keep an eye out for you. Good luck.'

Ritchie waited until the three of them were hidden from his view by a bend in the arroyo before putting a shredded-ended cheroot in his mouth and lighting it. He knew it was a wild-card scheme, but it stuck in his craw to give a greaser *bandido* all their heads on a plate. With the dynamite sticks held in his right hand he led his horse along the arroyo, his searching gaze from beneath the brim of his hat scanning both rims.

They were close; he could smell the bastards. Then he saw the tip of a high-crowned hat and the glint of a rifle barrel.

The sweat poured out of him. Don't go off a half-cock, Ritchie, he told himself, you've got time. They'll wait until they have four riders in their trap.

Five more yards into the ambushcade and he calculated he could win no more time for his *compadres*, the *bandidos* would know he was on his own and gun him down. Ritchie dropped the reins and turned his horse to shield himself from the ambushers as he touched off both fuses. Stepping back he threw them high, one on either rim of the arroyo. He heard screams and yells above the noise of the explosions and saw two bodies come hurtling backwards down the bank as he leapt into his saddle. His frightened horse took off in a wild-eyed, high-kicking gallop, threatening to unseat him as he clung low across its back.

Rifle fire opened up behind him and his horse gave a loud choking cough and blood gushed out of its mouth. It managed a few stumbling strides then its front legs gave way, throwing Ritchie clear over its head. He landed heavily and painfully, hitting his head on a stone that almost made him black out. He only dimly felt the added pain of being kicked and punched as he was dragged upright, unresistingly.

Mart heard the explosions and looked across at Guereca riding beside him. 'Our *amigo* has done what he set out to do, Señor Guereca,' he said. 'You and Panchito keep goin' to the mountains; I'll wait here for Ritchie. He could need some help if the sonsuvbitches are pressing him hard.'

'It is wise for the three of us to stay, Señor Langley,' Guereca said. 'All of El Lobo's band could have been waiting for us in the arroyo.'

Mart didn't try to dissuade the old man from staying. If Ritchie was being chased by twenty or so *bandidos*, three rifles could hold them off long enough for the four of them to reach the safety of the mountains. His one rifle would be a useless sacrifice. They would stamp him into the ground.

'OK, *compadres*,' he said. 'The three of us stay.' He grinned.

'But our *amigo* won't like it, he told us to wait for him in the mountains.'

The three of them pulled up their mounts, turning them round to watch for the fast-moving dust trail of a single rider. After a minute or two, on seeing no signs of Ritchie, Mart took out his army glasses to see if he could pick out any movement far out to his right, the way Ritchie would have to come if he had to swing real wide of the ambushers.

He gave the flat a long sweeping look, but the only glimmer of movement he saw was a distant shimmering heat-haze. 'Nothin',' he muttered, more to himself than at Guereca. He focused the glasses on to the line of the arroyo, beyond the spot where they had come out. He gave a sharp intake of breath. 'There's four of the sonsuvbitches comin' out of the arroyo, Señor Guereca! They're draggin' Ritchie along with them! He's still alive, thank God! They're headin' for those trees, the horses must be there.'

Mart lowered the glasses and looked at the old Mexican. 'They ain't goin' to come chasin' us, not when there's only four of them. It looks as though some of the ambushers have no need for their horses any more, Ritchie's dynamite must have put paid to some of them. We could try some ambushin' of our own, but that could get Ritchie killed. I reckon they'll be takin' him to El Lobo. You said it would be a good idea for a cattle-thief to hunt down another cattle-thief. Well, it's workin'.' Mart smiled, slightly. 'Though not in the way Ritchie would have favoured.' His face hardened again. 'Nor the way I would have wanted.

'There's only one way to play it now: trail

the bastards until we get to where El Lobo is and take what chances we can to rescue Ritchie and kill El Lobo!'

Sixteen

By craning his neck slightly, Ritchie could see they were heading for a village, then he quickly went limp again to fool his captors. Though it seemed as though a mule was trying to kick its way out of his head, and his ribs ached from the rough handling the *bandidos* had given him, he was still capable of using any breaks that came his way, haul himself out of the big hole he had landed in. If that wasn't possible, then he would try his damnedest to pull El Lobo down to hell with him. No way was he going to let the son-of-a-bitch have the last laugh on him.

Ritchie had one last wild card to play, a joker, a single stick of dynamite still in one piece, stuck in the top of his boots, and hidden by the leg of his pants. He firmly believed he had the time to play it. El Lobo, he opined, wouldn't kill out of hand. He would want to question him to find out exactly what he was up against. All he had to do was discover how he could pull out the stick with his hands tied behind his back in front of a bunch of hair-triggered *bandidos*.

Ritichie gave a wry grin. If things got desperate he could go out in real glory-boy style by throwing himself on some fire and kill as many of the bastards as he could. Being an owlhoot, he had expected to die violently, by the bullet or the rope. He wasn't going to die inch by agonizing inch at El Lobo's hands. When El Lobo found out as well as killing his men Ritchie had helped to destroy his stronghold, he could end up like the poor son-of-a-bitch stretched across the supply wagon's wheel. It was definitely less painful to be blown to Hell and beyond by a stick of dynamite.

His captors pulled up their horses outside a *cantina*. Ritchie recognized it as where they had begun making El Lobo pay off some of the debt he owed them, in the blood of his men. Hot rods shot through his chest as he was dragged off the horse. He gasped with pain and didn't have to fake unsteadiness.

Prodded in the back by the *bandido* whose horse he had been slung across, Ritchie staggered the few paces to the *cantina* porch and found himself facing a small, paunch-bellied Mexican wearing a faded, sweat- and food-stained army uniform. What he lacked in height, he made up with in weapons: three pistols, sheathed in bandoliers draped across his body, a machete slung at his waist, and a quirt held in his right hand. He had a mean-eyed, vicious-looking face. El Lobo, Ritchie opined, was rightly named. If he'd had the choice he would have rather faced a four-legged wolf.

Jose began to tell his *jefe* of the killing of his men by dynamite. 'By this gringo dog here,' he said jabbing Ritchie in the back with his rifle. 'Allowing his three *compadres* to escape.'

Ritchie noticed a nervous tic appear on El Lobo's right cheek, and flecks of saliva bubbling at the corners of his mouth as he was hearing the bad news. He was gazing into the red-flecked eyes of one mad wolf and knew waiting for the break-time he was banking on, wasn't a sure thing. El Lobo was crazy enough right now to gun him down in the next few seconds.

Then Jose told El Lobo about the explosions he had heard in the mountains and for once, El Lobo, a man who had instilled fear and terror in the souls of the villagers of Chihuahua, felt the chill of fear himself. Ritchie saw it flicker at the back of El Lobo's eyes. In spite of his pain, and knowing he was only a hair's-breadth away from death, he smiled inwardly. Me and the boys are getting at you, you murdering son-of-a-bitch, he thought with some joy. If you knew that two of them are Mexs, one no more than a young kid, then you would be getting real chewed-up inside.

Who are these gringos? El Lobo thought wildly, who are running rings round them and killing his *muchachos* where and when they liked? He angry-eyed the gringo in front of him to see if he could read the answer in him. If they had destroyed his stronghold all was lost to them. His band couldn't winter in the mountains without food and shelter. And there was no hiding place for them here on the plains from the Federale and Rurale patrols. His band would melt away, his power to get his wherewithal for free, gone. El Lobo let out a snarling cry of frustration. Savagely, he struck out with his quirt at one of the hated gringos responsible for his misfortunes.

Ritchie rocked back on his heels with pain as the whip slashed a knife-like cut across his left cheek. Somehow he controlled his temper. If he hadn't known that the man behind would shoot him down, he would have jumped on to the porch and tried to

154

kick El Lobo to death. He consoled himself with the thought that, if not him, then Langley or the old man, or Panchito, would see that El Lobo caught the fast, one-way train to Hell.

'You and your men, Jose, guard the gringo well,' El Lobo spat out. 'I will ride to the stronghold with the rest of the band to see if the other gringos have been there with their dynamite. Tie this dog out in the sun up against that fence. If his *compadres* come here to rescue him, shoot him in the stomach.' El Lobo gave Ritchie a bare-toothed, merciless grin. 'You will be lucky, gringo, the pain will not last long. If you're alive when I return, your mother, if she is dead, will feel your agony in her grave.'

Jose, not wanting the Yankees to cause him to lose face again or his *jefe* might not be so forgiving next time, positioned his men carefully after El Lobo had left the village. He placed a man on the bell tower of the church from where he had clear sightings of all the trails to the village, another at the window of the *cantina*. He and his last man, after tying their prisoner to one of the fence stakes of the sheep pen, took up posts on the flat roof of a store at the side of the pen. Four rifles were now covering the gringo.

155

Jose gave a smile of satisfaction. If the other gringos showed up they would only be attempting to rescue a dead man.

Eva Marie's hands had flown to her mouth to stifle her sobbing gasp on seeing the four *bandidos* riding in with one of Panchito's gringo *compadres* as a prisoner, fearing, tearfully, that her saviour and his two *amigos* were killed. Her hopes rose slightly when El Lobo and most of his men rode out and the four *bandidos* left behind, carrying rifles, hid themselves in buildings around the gringo standing roped to the post. It looked as though they were setting a trap for his *compadres* so some of them must still be alive. She had to put all wishful thoughts of who could still be alive from her mind and think of a way she could warn the tall Texan that he was riding into danger if he tried to rescue his *amigo*.

Mart, sitting higher in the saddle, saw the dust of several riders heading in their direction fast. They had left the arroyo and were trailing fast and openly across country, knowing the longer Ritchie was in El Lobo's hands the greater the chances of him ending up dead. Although there was need of urgency in their action, Mart wasn't taking any undue risks with his own life and the lives of his *compadres*. All of them getting killed wouldn't help Ritchie.

They knew were the men who had taken Ritchie were heading for, so he had let them ride on until they were out of sight before they began to trail them. Dust raised on the flat could be seen for miles and he figured Ritchie's captors, who'd had some of their *amigos* killed, would keep a nervous but watchful eye on their back-trail for signs of any threat to them.

Mart pointed to his left. 'In there!' he shouted, and the three of them guided their mounts in a haunch-sliding rush to the bottom of a dried-up water-hole. Mart slipped off his horse and scrambled back up to the edge with his army glasses in his hand.

The thick haze of drifting dust kicked up by the horses made it difficult for Mart to count the number of riders but he estimated there were at least fifteen. All of El Lobo's band, he thought, hightailing it back to their stronghold, to get one hell of a disappointment. He couldn't see any signs of Ritchie slung across any horse's back and had to fear the worst: they would find a dead Ritchie in San Ramon. Mart came down from the rim to tell Guereca and Panchito the bad news. A few minutes later, they rode out of the dip, grim-faced, dedicated, after they had paid their last respects to their dead *amigo* and seen him decently buried, to draw more blood from El Lobo in payment of his death.

Ritchie felt like hell. He was slowly frying to death, standing hatless in the full glare of the late afternoon sun. The quirt cut, a constant, painful throb, was attracting the flies and every time he shook his head to drive them off he had the extra agony of his head wound to bear. Buried up to his neck in an anthill, Ritchie thought, morbidly, would come as a great relief.

The dynamite in his right boot was still unbroken, the *bandidos* having only tied his hands and body to the stake, opining, Ritchie figured, that tying their prisoner's legs to the stake would have been a waste of sweat, knowing they would have him covered with four rifles all the time. Their carelessness in not finding the dynamite could, so he hoped, have some part in their downfall.

Ritchie knew it would only be a matter of time before Langley and his Mexican *amigos* showed up to effect his rescue. The ex-

Ranger wouldn't take long to spot where the riflemen were and deal with them. How they could do that without one of the *bandidos* plugging him, Ritchie hadn't worked out yet. He managed a ghost of a smile. In Texas, as a Ranger, Langley had risked his life several times to run him down and see him hang for cattle-lifting; now in this dog-dirt Mex village, the long-faced sonuvabitch was risking it again to save him from death.

The *bandido* in the *cantina* came across occasionally to give him a drink of brackish-tasting water. Ritchie knew it wasn't out of the goodness of his heart but to make sure he was still alive when El Lobo came back, so the chief could work on him with his knife.

Eva Marie lay flat on the ridge overlooking the main trail from the mountains, along which, she prayed anxiously, Panchito and his *compadres* would soon be riding.

She had been thinking, frantically, all afternoon of how she could help Panchito and his *compadres* to escape the trap. It was not until she saw the women going to the stream carrying their bundles of washing an idea came to her. All she had to do was to persuade her father to agree with her plan and unbolt the doors and let her leave the house.

There had been no time for Eva Marie to flee to the safety of the old dwellings when El Lobo and his band had ridden into the village, so her father had locked the doors of the house and told her to keep away from the windows. Although she knew that if she suffered the same terrible experience of being attacked by one of the *bandidos*, there would be no Panchito to come to her aid, Eva Marie watched, and worried, about what was happening to the Texan. Her father wouldn't let her out of the house at first, saying it was too dangerous for her to be seen in the square.

'How can there by any risk, Papa?' she had said. 'There are only four *bandidos* left in the village and they are guarding the Texan. And I'll be amongst the women going down to the stream. The guards won't see me going on to the south ridge, and from there I will be able to see the tall Texan and his *compadres* approaching the village.'

Eva Marie could see that her father wasn't convinced it was wise for her to leave the house. 'Did you not tell the tall gringo you owed him a great debt, Papa, for saving your daughter from being ravished? What debt do you think I owe Panchito then?'

Reluctantly her father gave his permission for her to go and try and warn the boy and the Texan of the danger, aware that the honour of his family owed them that, and more. He gave Eva Marie his blessing and a heavy pistol, that had belonged to the *bandidos* the Texans had killed in the village.

'Do not hesitate to use it on any of the dogs who try to molest you, Eva Marie,' he said. 'But if you do, do not come back to the village or his *compadres* will kill you. Go and hide in the old dwellings.'

'If I recall,' Mart said to Guereca, 'San Ramon lies just over that ridge up ahead.'

He had hardly spoken the words when he heard Panchito give out one of his gurgling warning cries and startled him by leaping off his horse and dropping down into an arroyo to his left and speed along it. 'The durn kid's seen something on that ridge, Señor Guereca,' he said. 'Though we're well outa rifle range, I think it would be wise for us to get ourselves outa sight.'

Eva Marie gave a cry of joy and raised herself on to her knees. Panchito was alive, she could see three riders coming along the trail towards her. When she looked again the

161

trail was deserted. Puzzled, she wondered if she had been wishing so hard to see Panchito and his *compadres* she had imagined she had seen them. Disappointed, she dropped back on to the ground again to continue her vigil.

Panchito paused for a minute or two just below the spine of the ridge to get his breathing back to normal, an Apache tactic. A man's laboured breathing could alert an enemy of his approach and lose him the advantage of an easy kill. Panchito had only taken twenty loping strides along the ridge when he stopped suddenly in his tracks. His fierce killing grimace changed into a surprised grin. His eyes hadn't played him false; there was someone on the ridge; he could see a pair of legs. Not the pants and spurred-booted legs of a *bandido* but the thigh-length smooth, brown limbs of a young *señorita*. Panchito lowered his machete.

Eva Marie, sensing someone was standing behind her, twisted round in alarm, the pistol held in a hand that shook. Then, seeing it was Panchito, she was on her feet again in a flash and threw her arms around him, laughing and crying as she hugged him tight. 'You're alive!' she sobbed.

Eva Marie's embrace came so suddenly and unexpectedly, Panchito just held his arms down by his side. Then, as the warm soft curves of her body got to him, he dropped the machete and wrapped his arms around her, pulling her closer to him.

Eva Marie drew slightly away from him and told him the reason for her being on the ridge. 'Your gringo *amigo* is alive, Panchito,' she said. 'But is being held prisoner by four *bandidos*. I will show the tall gringo where they are. They are the only ones in the village; El Lobo has left with the rest of his butchers.'

Then, suddenly, Eva Marie no longer wondered why Panchito had never spoken to her. She could see the reason by the anguish and frustration in his eyes. She had heard talk in the village that Panchito's bravery and fierceness in killing the *bandido* who had attacked her was because he had lived among the Apache and she knew that the blood-thirsty savages sometimes cut out their prisoners' tongues.

With a deep feeling of love and compassion, a sweet-smiling Eva Marie leaned forward and kissed Panchito, softening the look in his eyes. She took hold of his hand. 'Come, *mi hombre*, let us go and tell the tall

163

gringo that his *amigo* lives.'

Screened by a patch of high-standing mesquite, Mart and Guereca, cocked rifles in their hands, kept a watchful gaze on the ridge.

'That boy's keenness to blood his machete will get him killed one day,' Mart growled.

'Do not worry, Señor Langley,' the old Mexican replied. 'Remember the boy's mostly Apache, and they are not *hombres* who run blindly into trouble.'

'Yeah, I suppose you're right,' Mart said. 'But as you know I want the boy to have a future other than slittin' bad-asses' throats. If I...' He grinned at Guereca. 'Why, the young hellion's comin' off the ridge with that *señorita* he's kinda sweet on. I wonder what she's doin' there?'

Seventeen

Mart was doing some hard thinking, of how they could kill four riflemen before they gunned down Ritchie.

They were lying prone in a drainage ditch that ran across the rear of the sheep pen and could see Ritchie, leastways his back, and the buildings where Eva Marie had said the *bandidos* were. And there was another worry for Mart to contend with: the girl was in the ditch with them. Eva Marie had insisted that she had every right to help to kill the *bandidos*. Wasn't she under threat of being raped every time the *bandidos* came to the village? she had told him. And, putting her arm through Panchito's, had said, 'I stand alongside my *hombre*.' Panchito just grinned at him as though he was taking the girl to a village baile.

He had cast an exasperated look at Guereca, seeking his advice. The old Mexican had merely shrugged and muttered something about 'Mexican honour'. And who the hell was he, a Texas gringo, he

165

thought, to defy a Mexican working out his or her honour?

Mart thought he was coming up with a glimmer of a plan and talked it over with Guereca and Panchito.

'I can bring down the man in the bell tower easy enough,' he began. 'And both of you can tackle the two on the roof, force them to keep their heads down at least until I can free Ritchie. It's the bastard in the *cantina* who's the problem. We can't get at him and he's in the best position to shoot Ritchie, and he'll do just that once we open up.' Mart thought for a while before speaking again. 'Unless one of us can sneak into the *cantina* and kill him without his *compadres* on the roof catching on to the fact that their trap has lost a few teeth.' He looked at Guereca. 'You pulled a sneaky-like trick back there to get us into the stronghold, can you come up with another one, *amigo*?'

To their surprise it was Eva Marie who came up with a plan. 'I can get Panchito into the *cantina* without raising the *bandido's* suspicions, Señor Langley,' she said. She gazed proudly at Panchito. 'Panchito will then be able to kill the *bandido* silently with his machete.' Eva Marie, on seeing Mart's doubtful, worried face, smiled. 'There will be no danger to us, Señor Langley,' she said. 'The *bandido* will only see a boy and a girl carrying in a crate of wine. I do it every day; my father owns the *cantina*.'

That was not the way Mart was seeing it, though he did think the girl's plan could work. Some of the plans he had come up with didn't look so good at first, but they had got them breathing down El Lobo's neck, unharmed, so far. They had no time to come up with another plan to try and put off Eva Marie from taking a risk with her life; it would soon be dark and Ritchie would be taken indoors, making the chance of rescuing him that much harder.

'OK, *amigos*,' he said. 'Let's get things rollin'. I reckon Ritchie ain't feelin' so comfortable roped up to that stake. Here's what I want you to do, Panchito. Explain it to him, Eva Marie, if he doesn't understand all of it.'

The man at the *cantina* window swung round on his stool when Eva Marie and Panchito came through the rear door carrying a crate of wine between them. Eva Marie had eased the straps of her dress off her shoulders and loosened the top two buttons. Even in the fading light the *bandido* caught the tantalizing glimpse of the round fullness of barely concealed breasts.

'We are only bringing in some wine for my father, *señor*,' Eva Marie said, gaze downcast.

The *bandido* grinned. The girl had brought something in more blood-stirring than a few bottles of wine. He laid down his rifle and got up from his stool and walked across to the pair, thinking that after he had booted the boy out of the *cantina*, the girl would help to pass a cold night more pleasantly. He took the last two steps in his life. With his eyes and senses inflamed with lust this close to the girl, he didn't notice the boy moving round to the side of him.

The hate inside Panchito was burning him up. As well as killing the man for being a *bandido* he was killing him for violating his woman with his lewd gaze. With a silent victory snarl, Panchito swung his machete. Eva Marie turned her head away as the blade sliced across the *bandido's* throat and heard him drop heavily on to the floor.

Panchito stood over him until he heard his last shuddering gasp for breath. He picked up the dead man's sombrero and put it on then motioned to Eva Marie to stay where she was and to keep low. He crossed to the window to show himself to the *bandidos* on the roof opposite, raising the sombrero twice as he sat down on the stool.

An anxious-waiting Mart saw the agreed signal that it had gone as planned in the *cantina*, and grinned his relief at Guereca. He had lost sight of Panchito and the girl since leaving the ditch, but Eva Marie had shown that, as young and pretty as she was, she could play her part alongside any *hombre* in a tight situation and be found not wanting. 'OK, Señor Guereca,' he said. 'Go and get yourself some sheep.'

A pain-racked Ritchie saw the old man driving a bunch of sheep coming in from his right, some of the animals close enough to brush past his legs. There was still sufficient spirit left in him to demonstrate the cattleman's loathing for woollies by kicking out at them and snarling a curse at their drover. The drover favoured him with a moon-faced grin, and if Ritchie had been a crying man he would have shed tears of joy. The mournful-faced sonuvabitch, Langley, and his two *amigos* hadn't given up on him.

He guessed that the ex-Ranger had figured out where the all the *bandidos* were and had sent the kid and his deadly wielded machete to deal with the man in the *cantina*,

169

old Guereca's targets were the two bastards on the roof. Against his long held prejudices, Ritchie was getting a liking for Mexicans.

Mart covered the two men on the roof while Guereca unfastened the gate of the pen, ready to take them on if they made a hostile move against the old Mexican as he was rounding up his herd of sheep. Seeing that Guereca was in no danger, Mart drew a bead on the man in the bell tower, finger taking up the slack on the trigger as he waited for the old sheep herder to start the killing.

As the sheep passed below him, a grinning Jose leant over the edge of the roof and called out, 'Hey, old fart, when you get those sheep to the water you tell one of those *señoras* to bring me and my *compadre* a bottle of wine, pronto!'

'You and your *compadre* won't need any wine in hell, *amigo*,' Guereca said softly, and drew back a corner of his serape and brought his rifle up and fired it from the hip.

The shell caught the surprised Jose full in the face, shattering the back of his head into a bloody mess of bone and tissue. His *compadre* moved back quickly from the edge, out of sight of the old Mexican who wasn't a sheepman at all who had just blown out Jose's brains, only to find himself under fire from the *cantina* window, where Valdez should have been. He flung himself flat on to the roof to shelter behind the low parapet that ran along the front of the building from the deadly fire. Ignoring El Lobo's orders to kill the gringo prisoner if they came under attack, he began to inch his way backwards towards the rear of the roof, to drop off and run for his horse and ride out of the village before the gringos started using their dynamite. Staying alive suited him better than dying trying to carry out his *jefe's* orders.

On hearing Guereca's shot, Mart fired as fast as he could work the Winchester's lever. He ceased firing when he saw the man in the tower drop his unfired rifle and fall to the ground like some gigantic bird of prey diving for its intended victim, his piercing scream snapping off when he hit the ground with a dust-raising thud. Mart brought his rifle round in time to put two shells in the back of the last *bandido* as he was dropping down from the roof, ending all opposition against them. He got to his feet. 'OK, *amigos*!' he yelled. 'It's all done!'

Panchito and Eva Marie came out of the *cantina*. Panchito ran across to Ritchie and cut him free. Ritchie groaned and leant heavily on the boy or he would have keeled over. He saw the girl and gave a lopsided grin. 'Jesus!' he muttered. 'Langley will be recruitin' them from the cradle next. Panchito,' he said, 'if I ever make it back across the Rio Grande, I'll promise you this: if I hear any Texan call Mexicans greasers I'll plug him in the foot.'

Mart grimaced when he saw the weals on Ritchie's face. 'Let's get you inside and clean out those wounds with whiskey or they'll turn bad on you. And I'd be obliged, Señor Guereca, if you and Panchito will collect up the dead *bandidos*' guns, and hide the bodies.' His face steeled over. 'We're goin' to take on El Lobo and what's left of his gang here in San Ramon: we're finished chasin' after him. We've got the edge here. When he comes back he'll not expect us to be where his boys were. And the sons-of-bitches won't know that until our lead's cuttin' them down.'

With a struggle, Ritchie pulled up his pants leg and took out the stick of dynamite from his boot. He managed a pitiful grin. 'I was keepin' this little beauty for El Lobo,' he said. 'I'll get a chance tomorrow to throw it into his ugly face. Now, let me get into that *cantina* and get some of that whiskey you're goin' to clean my cuts with down my throat as well, where it will do most good.'

Señor Gomez was in the *cantina* watching his daughter cleaning the wounds of the fat gringo who was biting his lip to hold in his curses, as the whiskey on his open wound stung as painfully as the quirt lashes had.

Gomez was angry with his daughter for risking her life and yet proud of her. He had been disappointed at not having a son but no son could have acted so bravely as Eva Marie had. Though, by the way she had been smiling at Panchito when they came out of the *cantina*, he opined he would soon have a son-in-law. As a man of honour he had to accept his daughter's choice. Without the boy's bravery he wouldn't have had a daughter to worry over. And seeing a new, bolder, more headstrong side to his daughter, Gomez knew he wouldn't be allowed a say in choosing a husband.

When Guereca and Panchito returned laden with the *bandido's* guns and shell belts, there were several villagers standing outside the *cantina* busy discussing, with much arm-waving and raised voices, the latest shooting down of El Lobo's men and what their fate would be when the *bandido*

173

jefe returned to San Ramon.

Guereca gave them a contemptuous glare. Señor Langley was a man too proud to ask for help in what he thought was a private war with El Lobo for killing his wife. A mistaken thought, in Guereca's opinion. The fight against the *bandidos* should have been taken up by every villager in northern Chihuahua. It was their faces El Lobo was grinding in the dirt.

He flung the guns and the ammunition down at their feet and nodded to Panchito to do the same and began to harangue them for being spineless *hombres*.

'Are you just going to sit on your arses?' he snarled at them. 'Praying to the Holy *Madre* while watching El Lobo and his butchers rape your wives and daughters?' Then Guereca twisted the truth somewhat. 'I, a man old enough to be your grandfather, and this young boy here, helped by my two Texan *amigos*, have destroyed El Lobo's stronghold and killed over half of his men!' He pointed to the weapons on the ground. 'With these guns and the ones Señor Langley gave you, you can arm more men than El Lobo has. And as you have seen, *bandidos* can easily be killed.'

'I will take a rifle, Señor Guereca,' Gomez

said, as he came out of the *cantina*. 'I am not a brave *hombre*, but I can't let my daughter fight battles I should fight.'

'*Bueno*, Señor Gomez,' Guereca said, still eyeing the rest of the villagers angrily.

He saw them exchange glances and mutter together. Then, one of them stepped forward. 'Do not shame us any further, *amigo*,' he said. 'We will fight alongside you and your gringo *compadres*.'

Guereca beamed and embraced the spokesman. 'The names of the villagers of San Ramon will be known and honoured throughout the whole of Mexico as the slayers of the Wolf of Chihuahua. The Governor of Chihuahua will send you gold in recognition of your bravery. Give them their guns, Panchito, I'll go and tell Señor Langley he is the *generale* of an army.' In a lower voice, he added, 'Make sure the "soldiers" don't shoot themselves with the guns, *amigo*.'

Eighteen

El Lobo was convinced El Diablo had laid a curse on him. How else was it possible for four *hombres* to have killed so many of his *muchachos* and destroy his stronghold? He was riding back to San Ramon with what was left of his once powerful band to question his prisoner. El Lobo's face twisted in demonic rage. The gringo dog would tell him about his *compadres* who carried dynamite, in between his screams of pain.

On seeing the blocked-off pass to the stronghold he had ordered two of his men to climb their way round the rock tumble and check on things at the stronghold. It had taken over two hours of impatient waiting for the pair to come back down the mountain, exhausted, with hands and knees bleeding, with the fearful news that the stronghold had been destroyed and only the dead and the badly wounded were left there.

El Lobo had to concentrate his thoughts on the tortures he was going to inflict on his prisoner or he would have gunned down the bringers of the bad news just to ease some of his rage at how bad his luck was running. That, he knew, would be foolish and dangerous for him. He could see his men were touchy and nervous and would not take kindly to him shooting two of their *compadres* for reasons which were not their fault, and he needed every gun he had to fight the gringo dynamiters.

After a cold, restless night camp where taut nerves imagined every wind-rustling brush was a gringo dynamiter closing in on the camp, on going round, roughly toeing his men awake, El Lobo discovered that six of his men had sneaked out of the camp during the night. After cursing them for being cowardly dogs, he realized how wise he had been not to have shot the two men. If he had let his temper rule him he could still be lying on his blanket, having had his throat cut by the new *jefe*.

'Mount up, *muchachos*,' he said and noticing their surly looks, added, 'There'll be hot food, wine and hot women for the taking at San Ramon, and a gringo dog who will be made to pay for the deaths of our *compadres*.'

Mart had made his preparations for the

final showdown with El Lobo. He had more men than he could arm. Every man in the village had lined up outside the *cantina* clamouring for a gun so they could take part in the shedding of the cursed El Lobo's and his mad dogs' blood, none of them wanting to be branded as a coward by their neighbours.

By working most of the night, womenfolk included, a trench had been dug inside the sheep pen facing the *cantina*, so that five men, commanded by Guereca, would have some shelter from the *bandidos'* return fire, and from the cross-fire of their three *compadres* in the *cantina*, Panchito's detail. Mart had to remember that these men weren't Texas Rangers used to firing guns and being under fire: they would be scared and firing wild. At both ends of the killing ground, men warned that the *bandidos* were on their way, would hide behind the broken adobe walls of deserted buildings with strict orders from their gringo *generale*, not to fire or show themselves unless the *bandidos* broke and tried to hightail it out of the village their way.

Ritchie would start what Mart was banking on would be a massacre. He didn't want the villagers involved in a long drawn-out gunfight; that kind of action increased the risk of some of them getting killed or wounded. Ritchie's dynamite stick and the wall of fire on both sides of the *bandidos* would be so unexpected and blood shedding it should unnerve them enough, so he hoped, to break them before they got over the shock of riding into a trap and returned their fire.

The raiders splashed their way across the stream, all wary-eyed, and with drawn rifles held across saddle horns ready for instant use. El Lobo was getting the uncomfortable feeling that the most feared band of hunters in northern Mexico had now become the hunted. The quietness of the village increased that uneasiness until he saw Jose, squatting in the bell tower, raise his rifle in a greeting to him. El Lobo's screwed-up nerves began to unwind a little.

El Lobo paid no heed to the two men in the sheep pen, nor to the *cantina* owner carrying crates into the *cantina* but the sight of his gringo prisoner still tied to the post brought a smile to his face, the first for days. When he worked on the gringo with his knife, his screams would wake up the whole village.

As the *bandidos* rode beneath Mart,

wearing the dead Jose's poncho and sombrero, he somehow resisted the strong
temptation to just put a Winchester shell
through the head of the squat, mean-faced
man dressed in an old Federale officer's
uniform. But he owed it to the villagers of
San Ramon, who were putting their lives on
the line, to see that all of the *bandidos* paid
the ultimate penalty for all their killing and
raping. One shot and the band would
scatter, to live and be able to carry on with
their killing.

On first seeing the trail dust of the raiders,
Mart had stood up and waved both arms,
warning his 'troops' the enemy was in sight
and it was time they took up their firing
positions. Guereca and three of his men
slipped down into the trench, lying flat on
the bottom while the other two men laid
straw across the digging to conceal it, and to
prevent the sheep from falling in. To El
Lobo, it would seem as though two men
were checking on their sheep, a normal
village chore.

Gomez had placed several crates outside
the *cantina* door ready to look busy when
the *bandidos* showed up. He made sure the
door of the *cantina* was jammed open for
him to hurl himself through before the

181

dynamite exploded, and then take his place at one of the windows to try and kill himself a *bandido*. Gomez now knew the reason why Panchito couldn't speak, but had ceased puzzling over how a son-in-law, with no tongue, could help to run a *cantina*; he was more concerned with the depressing thought that in a few minutes he would be beyond worrying about anything for ever, at least this side of his grave.

Not having much confidence in his and the rest of the villagers' fighting capabilities, Gomez knew his life would lie in the hands of Panchito, tongueless or not, and his three *compadres*, the expert slayers. So, being a man of honour, and not wanting to lose his daughter's affections, he could look nothing less than favourably on Panchito as a son-in-law.

Ritchie stood head-drooped, sagging at the knees, like a man played out by his ordeal. The rope across his chest was tied in a slip knot, and his hands behind his back were untied. One held a tip glowing cheroot, the other, the last stick of dynamite, the fuse shortened to a four-second burn.

Ritchie kept his gaze lowered as El Lobo and his band drew up their horses in front of the *cantina*. In spite of the pain from his cuts and bruises, his lips drew back in an all-toothed genuine grin as he touched off the fuse. He heard its spluttering and brought his hand round fast and lobbed it at the *bandidos*.

'That's for some good Texas boys, you bastards!' he yelled, as he threw himself down to his left, landing painfully behind a stone water tank, and his rifle, as the dynamite exploded.

Panchito saw the stick arcing through the air and motioned for his men to get down from the windows and lie flat on the floor, being well acquainted with the destructive power of dynamite.

Gomez almost left it too late to dash back into the *cantina* when he saw Ritchie throw the dynamite. The blast caught him as he was going through the door – sending him flying into the room. He caught his head on the edge of a table, hard enough for him to black out for a few moments. By the time he came round, and got to his feet and picked up his rifle to take up his post at the window, El Lobo's band was no more. The dynamite had done its deadly work.

Horses and men struck by the flying stones went down in a mêlée of tangled bodies, screaming with pain. The rest, blinded by the dust, clung on to their rearing mounts with both hands to stay seated, unable to bring their guns into play. The gunfire from the *cantina* and the fire trench, though ragged in comparison to volleys fired by trained troops, was heavy enough to sweep them out of their saddles, dead several times over.

El Lobo was lucky, for the moment. His horse fell sideways, flinging him clear, up against the wall of the *cantina*. Its body sheltered him from the fire from the sheep pen and he was too low on the ground for the riflemen in the *cantina* to bring their guns to bear on him. Sobbing with fear and rage, he used the bodies of his men and the horses as cover to crawl to the side of the *cantina*, away from the deadly hail of lead, then took to his heels to get out of San Ramon fast.

Mart saw him come running round the building, hat and rifle gone and brought up his rifle to his shoulder, pulling off a load. It wasn't a killing head shot. Now all the *bandidos* had been killed, he had time to get the satisfaction of hanging El Lobo. El Lobo howled like a kicked dog and dropped to the ground clutching at his right leg.

By the time Mart had come down from the tower and walked over to where he had brought down El Lobo, the *bandido jefe* was ringed in by the armed villagers, poking at him with their rifles, laughing and jeering at him, no longer afraid of the Wolf of Chihuahua.

'Any of our men wounded?' Mart asked Guereca.

'*Nada*,' the old man replied. 'They didn't live long enough to fire off a single shot. Your *hombres*, Señor Langley, have left El Lobo alive for you to have the pleasure of killing him. They know of the terrible things he and his men did to your family.'

Mart looked down at the scowling, pain-twisted face of El Lobo, the man he had sworn over his wife's grave to hunt down and kill. Yet his wife hadn't been the only woman to be butchered by El Lobo in Chihuahua. He gave El Lobo another dispassionate look then came to a decision.

'Señor Gomez,' he said, 'my wife was a Mexican and I opine she would think it only right that her own people should be the executioners of this dog. And who have more right than the brave *hombres* of San Ramon who have destroyed El Lobo's band. Hang him, Señor Gomez!' Mart suddenly

185

held up a hand. 'Hold on, *señor*,' he said, curtly, and called for his three *compadres* to come to his side.

'I reckon, El Lobo,' he said, 'you've been wonderin' just who the hell it was who's been killin' your boys and destroyed your hole-up. Well, you're gazin' on them now: two gringos, a Mexican old enough to be your pa, and a boy young enough to be your son. So you ain't such a wild wolf after all.' Mart favoured him with a mirthless smile. 'I figure that ain't a comfortin' thought to ponder on before these folk dispatch you to Hell.' Mart nodded to Gomez. 'He's all yours now.'

El Lobo jerked back on the ground as though he had been shot again, his eyes widening in disbelief. He had been doubly cursed, he thought. As the villagers grabbed hold of him and dragged him upright, face working with hatred, he did some cursing and dirty-mouthing of his own on the heads of the four *hombres* who had brought about his downfall.

Ritchie grinned at Mart. 'That's one helluva unhappy *hombre* about to meet his Maker.'

The villagers were having a grand baile,

having two events to celebrate. Their hanging of the Wolf of Chihuahua and engagement of Gomez's daughter to Panchito, the *bandido* slayer. Mart and Ritchie were sitting at a big sparking wood fire watching the dancers whirling around under the strings of coloured paper lanterns hanging from the trees.

'Have you told the kid about his windfall, Langley?' Ritchie said.

'Yeah,' replied Mart. 'He'll use some of it to buy a piece of land just south of here. It's part of some don's rundown estate. There's buildin's on it and, accordin' to old Guereca, it's good land for raisin' sheep on, and he oughta know. Him and Gomez are goin' to keep an eye on Panchito's finances. And Eva Marie, I opine, will teach her future husband his letters and numbers. Me and Gomez are riding down to Chihuahua City in the morning to see to all the legal papers. Panchito will do fine puttin' his roots down here; you can see by the way he's grinning he's doin' that.'

'And what do you intend doin'?' Ritchie asked.

'Me?' said Mart. 'I'm stayin' here in Mexico. All I have, alive and dead, are in Chihuahua. When I've got myself some supplies I'll try and track down the band of Apache who's got my boys. I should have asked El Lobo about them, but I was rarin' mad to see the sonuvabitch hang.' He gave Ritchie a quizzical look. 'And where are you bound for, *amigo*?'

'I might stay south of the Rio Grande as well,' Ritchie said. 'I can't lift cattle without a gang.' He grinned. 'I'm kinda gettin' a likin' for Mexicans, especially that purty, plump-assed *señorita* who's been rollin' her eyes at me for the last ten minutes.' He was still smiling when he said, 'Bein' that you gave the kid my gold I'm flat broke. If you could see your way clear to give me two squares a day I might be your pard on that trip you're makin'. Trackin' down wild red men must be a job for a coupla men, Langley.'

Mart looked at Ritchie in surprise, wondering if the ex-rustler was joshing him, but could see no signs of that in his face. 'It won't be a pleasure trip, Ritchie: you could get yourself killed.'

'Ain't I been tryin' to do that these past few weeks?' Ritchie retorted. 'And if I go back to Texas I could get myself dead there as well. Your old buddies in the Rangers, Langley, are waitin' for me, swingin' a hangin' rope in their hands.'

Mart didn't take long in thinking over Ritchie's offer; he needed all the help he could come up with, but a man didn't ask a friend if he was interested in riding to his possible death. Especially if he had just been riding along a similar trail.

Mart reached out and shook Ritchie's hand. 'You're hired, pard,' he said. 'It would be downright foolish of me not to accept the services of an expert dynamiter. Now, go and join in the shindig with that *señorita* you have a fancy for. If you sweet-talk to her she might allow you to spend the night with her.' He grinned. 'If her pa don't mind.' Mart got to his feet. 'I'm goin' to get some sleep. I ain't as young as I was and it's a long ride to Chihuahua City. I'll see you when I get back then we can start plannin' our next hunt.'

Mart thought he would sleep well tonight. He'd had bloody retribution for El Lobo's killing of his wife. If his luck still held out, he opined, there was a possibility he could be reunited with his sons.

This Large Print Book, for people
who cannot read normal print,
is published under the auspices of

THE ULVERSCROFT FOUNDATION

... we hope you have enjoyed this book.
Please think for a moment about those
who have worse eyesight than you ...
and are unable to even read or enjoy
Large Print without great difficulty.

You can help them by sending a
donation, large or small, to:

**The Ulverscroft Foundation,
1, The Green, Bradgate Road,
Anstey, Leicestershire, LE7 7FU,
England.**
or request a copy of our brochure for
more details.

The Foundation will use all donations
to assist those people who are visually
impaired and need special attention
with medical research, diagnosis
and treatment.

Thank you very much for your help.